I BOUGHT EVERY DREAM
HE SOLD ME 3

J. DOMINIQUE

I Bought Every Dream He Sold Me 3

Copyright © 2023 by J. Dominique

All rights reserved.

Published in the United States of America.

Mailing List

To stay up to date on new releases, plus get information on contests, sneak peeks, and more,

Go To The Website Below...

www.colehartsignature.com

PREVIOUSLY...
HEAVY

It was a week before Adore's first court date, and I could tell that the closer we got the more worried she became of what the outcome might be. Aside from keeping a close eye on her, I still had yet to get Hector to set up the meet with Black's hitman and I was starting to think he was doing the shit on purpose. Shit was really starting to make me look at him funny, but until he actually did something to cross me I wouldn't jump the gun.

I was in the middle of trying to get sleep, when my phone started jumping with back-to-back messages. Seeing Sha'ron's name instantly had me ready to cut the shit off. I still had Kay Kay since the day she'd let that goofy shit roll off her tongue in front of her and I had no intentions on taking her back any time soon. It hurt to see her going down such a spiral, but I wasn't going to help her until she decided she wanted the help. Reading the messages, I jumped up, careful not to wake Adore as I scrambled to throw on some sweats. Even as crazy as she had sounded the last time I saw her, I hadn't been too concerned, but the shit she'd just sent my phone had me on high alert.

I slipped out of the house quietly and jumped in my truck, grateful that she didn't live too far away. The whole way there I told myself I was being goofy for even trying to help her ass as I dialed her phone back-to-back with no answer. "Fuck!" I shouted, pounding my fist on the steering wheel. It felt like everybody was out slowing me down, when really it was only a few cars on the road. By the time I reached her block I was already pulling off my seatbelt so I could hop straight out, and that's exactly what I did, damn near wrecking her car as I pulled into her driveway. Just like the last time I was there, the radio was up loud as hell and, of course, the door was locked tight.

"Ronnie! Ronnie!" I shouted, kicking her door with force until it finally flew open, and the sight before me had my mind racing. Her apartment was tore the fuck up. There was glass and shit everywhere like a tornado had flown through, or somebody that was pissed off, which only had me more frantic. I checked every room on the first floor and came up empty, giving me a little bit of hope, but the second I stepped on the landing at the top of the stairs, my chest deflated. There was literally blood from the top of the stairs to the master bedroom smeared into the cream carpet. It looked like a horror movie, and despite the shit I'd done to niggas in the past, knowing that it was a good chance I was seeing my baby mama's blood had me sick. Against my better judgment, I followed the trail until I came to her body on the floor. Running over to her, I dropped down and cradled her bloody head. She was covered in scratches and bruises on every inch of her exposed skin.

"What the fuck, Ronnie! Hey, hey, wake up!" I shouted, slapping her cheek as she laid limply in my arms. It took me a few minutes to realize there was no way she'd done this to herself. My mind raced trying to think of who would've done some shit like that to her, and I drew a big ass blank. The sound of sirens gave me hope that maybe she could still be helped, and I gently laid her head back down so I could let them in. They stayed in a quiet neighborhood, so I was sure one of her nosy ass neighbors had heard what happened

and called the police. I made it down the stairs just as they kicked the door in. "She's upstairs—"

"Put your hands up and get on the floor!" A rush of officers stormed inside pointing guns and flashlights in my face, momentarily stunning me as I tried to tell them where Sha'ron was. "I said put your fuckin' hands up!"

"Look, my baby mama upstairs, somebody—"

"Shut the fuck up!" Before I could get another word out I was kicked in the leg, making me kneel as at least ten officers swarmed me barking different orders. Not trying to get shot, I raised my bloody hands up like they said and realized I must have looked like the person who'd come in and attacked Sha'ron. As one of the officers cuffed my hands behind my head, I noticed that none of them had even gone upstairs to check on my baby mama and I was pissed. They struggled to get me out the door as I continued to scream for somebody to get her. It seemed like every neighbor she had was standing outside watching as they shoved me in a squad car and carted my ass off to the police station.

I didn't know how much time had passed when the door to the interrogation room opened and two detectives shuffled in looking like they'd slept in their clothes. They were both white and looking at me with steely glares, and I assumed that was because of the dried blood covering my hands and arms. Goofy asses hadn't even given me a chance to clean myself up or shit. I watched them silently drop into the chairs across from me and folded my hands on top of the steel table.

"You ready to talk, Dominique?" the younger of the two asked. He looked like he'd just gotten out of training with his bare face and curly blond hair, and I instantly pegged him as the "good cop" with a smirk.

"Aye, I don't like the way his ass sayin' my name. Send somebody else," I said dryly, and he shot his partner a questioning look. His ass hadn't even mastered a poker face yet. The older one

who proved to be the "bad cop" slammed his hand down on the table.

"Cut the shit! Why did you kill Sharon!" he roared, leaning over and hovering in my face.

"I told you I ain't touch Sha'ron. I got text messages from her saying she was about to end it and some other crazy shit, so—"

"So, you decided to go over there and help her out?" he probed.

"Look, you lucky I'm even willin' to talk to y'all goofy asses. I told you what the fuck happened and I ain't sayin' shit else till my lawyer get here." I was done playing with them. They weren't trying to find out what happened anyway, they were trying to get my black ass to confess. He stared at me silently for a few seconds to intimidate me, but I was far from the weak ass niggas that shit usually worked on. I stared right back at his ass until he finally looked away, standing abruptly with his partner following right behind him. Sighing, I leaned back in my seat, knowing they didn't have shit on me but still being pissed by the inconvenience. My biggest issue was finding out how the fuck Sha'ron had gotten killed and who had the balls to do it.

The sound of the door squeaking open again snatched my attention away from my bloodstained hands, and I smirked at the sight of the mayor as he walked in looking smug.

"You had to come see for yourself, or you just bored as hell since you been fired?"

"Suspended, temporarily," he corrected, and my grin widened. If no one else could be considered delusional, it was definitely him and his lame ass son. "But yes, I came to see for my handywork for myself." This time it was his turn to grin as I realized what he was saying. "Smart, huh? You don't have to say it, I know."

"If it was so smart, then how the fuck you figure they gone be able to hold me for this bullshit ass charge! I can prove I wasn't nowhere around when that shit happened!" I growled, knowing that the only reason he was this close and talking this much shit was *because of our location. Outside those walls, he would never be so bold.*

"Ahhh, but I don't need them to hold you forever, just long enough to make my problem go away, and then I don't give a shit what you do." Shrugging, he released a supervillain laugh. "Next time, try a less worthy opponent than your father, son. I win every time," he cackled, strolling out the room.

To Be Continued...

CHAPTER ONE

ADORE

I woke up to Kay Kay bouncing on the bed and smiled groggily. Having a little girl around that was the same age as Kaliyah was bittersweet. While it warmed my heart that Heavy trusted me with her, it also made me yearn for my baby even more. I wondered if she jumped on Niko and Farrah's bed in the morning and my smile wilted a little.

"A-dore. Do. You. Know. Where. My. Daddy. Is?" Kay Kay's squeaky voice snatched me out of my spiraling thoughts as she bounced between each word. Confused, I looked over to his side of the bed and was surprised to see he wasn't there. Heavy usually let me know when he was leaving, so to see him gone and not remembering him waking me, I wasn't sure what to tell her. Not wanting to lie, I forced a smile and shrugged.

"I don't, but we can try to go find him. Maybe he's trying to play hide and seek with us?" Even as I said it the suggestion sounded stupid as hell, but it seemed to do the trick because she excitedly climbed out of bed and tried to pull me up too.

As usual, she was talking a mile a minute as I put on my robe and Heavy's Nike slides. Grabbing my phone, I followed her out into the hall, checking each room along the way. When we made it downstairs and still hadn't found him, I grew a little worried and called his phone. It immediately went to voicemail each of the five times I tried him, and although I had a funny feeling about what was going on, I tried to hide my concern.

"Well, maybe he went to run some errands. Let's make breakfast and hopefully he'll be back by the time we're done."

The look she gave me was doubtful, but she still accepted my hand, asking, "Can we make the confetti pancakes?"

"Yep, we can make them real fancy too, come on." We headed to the kitchen, with me discreetly texting Heavy with my free hand. Pushing my concern to the back of my mind, I tried to focus on helping her measure out each ingredient before adding it to the mixing bowl. She was just as meticulous as her grandma when it came to cooking and quickly got the swing of things, putting her skills to use.

We were just about to start pouring our batter into the pan when the doorbell rang. I gave Kay Kay a questioning look, but she only shrugged, not really caring since it wasn't likely her father. "Why don't you prep the eggs for me and I'll be right back," I told her, sitting the carton and another big bowl on the counter for her. Instantly, her eyes lit up and I regretted the decision, but it was too late to take it back. She went to work cracking eggs while I headed to the door, only to hear the unmistakable splat of one hitting the linoleum before I even rounded the corner. Wincing, I picked up speed, hoping that whoever it was wouldn't take too much of my time. I took the time to check my phone, like a message or call would've come through without me noticing, and rolled my eyes when I still came up empty. I was so caught up in my irritation, I didn't stop to check the peephole before pulling the door open.

"Oh, thank god!" Miss Pam exclaimed, grabbing me up into

a hug. "Where's Kaylani?" She was already moving past me in search of her granddaughter while I stood there confused.

"She's in the kitchen. What's going on, did something happen to Dominique?" My level of worry was already growing just from the way she was acting. She hurriedly came back over to where I was standing frozen and placed her hands on both my shoulders.

"Sha'ron was beaten damn near to death last night, and they arrested Dominique for it since he was there when the police came."

"Oh my god!" My heart instantly dropped to the pit of my stomach hearing that. I'd known something wasn't right about Heavy being MIA and suddenly, all of the sneaky suspicions I'd had made sense. Ms. Pam was still talking but my thoughts were racing with all types of questions. *Why had he gone to see his baby mama when Kay Kay was with us? When had he left? Had he really been the one that beat her up?*

"I need to get up there and find out what the fuck going on, 'cause something's not right! I know damn well my baby didn't do no shit like this!"

"I'm coming too."

"No!" she damn near shouted, pulling me back since I'd begun to walk off. "We don't need Kay Kay in no police station. You just stay here with her until I figure out what's going on." Just that quick, I'd forgotten all about Kay Kay. Ms. Pam was right, the police station was no place for her, and as bad as I wanted to go check on Heavy, I didn't want to traumatize her.

"Okay, I can do that, but please let me know as soon as you find out something," I managed to choke out on the verge of tears. This was a lot to take in and it was going to be hard to keep my cool in front of Kay Kay, but I managed to swallow down my emotions. Giving my hand a tight squeeze, she promised to do just that before rushing back out the door.

"What the fuck, Dominique," I sighed out loud, pressing my back against the door as I tried to make sense of this shit. A loud clatter snapped me out of my thoughts and I remembered I'd left Kay Kay in the kitchen. She was already calling my name before my feet even began to move, and I made it back just in time to see that she dropped the bowl of eggs and was busy wiping it up with paper towels.

"I was trying to stir it like the chefs do and it just fell," she immediately explained, seeing me in the doorway.

"It's okay baby, I got it," I told her, trying hard not to sob as I grabbed everything I would need to clean up the mess. Together we had the floor looking just as spotless as it had when we'd come down. Afterward, we finished making breakfast with her talking a mile a minute while I tried not to check my phone every few seconds for a word from Ms. Pam. Poor thing was completely oblivious to the fact that her mama was currently in the hospital fighting for her life and her daddy was behind bars for putting her there. I felt terrible sitting across from her as she ate, trying to pretend like everything was okay.

"Adore, are you okay? You look really sad, is it because my daddy isn't back yet?" She looked at me quizzically, holding a forkful of pancakes in midair with her head tilted. Caught off guard, I opened and closed my mouth a couple of times before emphatically shaking my head.

"Oh no, I'm just—" The doorbell ringing cut me off and I was actually thankful for the interruption. Withholding information and lying were two different things, and I found the latter to be much worse than keeping her in the dark about what was going on. "Uh, let me go get that." I hauled ass out of the kitchen, chastising myself the whole way to the door. I clearly needed to perk up or Kay Kay would get suspicious, and the last thing I wanted was to have her stressed out about her parents. Releasing a shaky breath, I paused to check the peephole this time before swinging the door open. I didn't immediately recognize the man standing before me, but I was more puzzled than afraid, until he pulled a gun from underneath his coat.

Although Heavy had warned me of the danger I was in, I hadn't had any reason to worry with him around, and now that he wasn't there to protect me a nigga was conveniently popping up. Instinctively, I attempted to shut the door back, but he wedged his booted foot inside and forced me backward.

"Aht, aht, not so fast, babygirl," he sneered, stepping in and closing the door behind himself.

"Look, I don't know what you want, but if you leave right now I promise I won't call the police or nothin'." Careful to keep my voice low so Kay Kay wouldn't hear what was going on, I backed away with my hands raised. My weak attempt to dissuade him did nothing but garner a snicker as he advanced on me.

"You funny, shorty. What makes you think you gone be able to call anybody by the time I leave?" He paused, briefly letting his eyes roam my body from head to toe, and I regretted not putting on some clothes upon getting up. "You know, the picture Mr. Black gave me didn't do you justice at all. You fine as fuck, for real. Maybe if you let me hit first I'll make this shit quick." His eyebrows rose with the suggestion, and I couldn't hide my disgust. Besides him basically discussing raping me, he was ugly as hell and his facial expressions only made it worse. However, instead of gagging like I wanted to, I quickly fixed my face and forced a look of fake hopefulness.

"Really?" His eyes lit up and I mentally added that he was stupid to his list of faults.

"Oh, fa sho." Without waiting for me to agree, he set his gun down on the entryway table and immediately began unfastening his jeans. As soon as his eyes were off me, I inched closer to table.

"Adoooooore, what's taking so long?" Kay Kay's voice quickly snatched both of our attention, and I took the opportunity to scoop up the vase next to me and throw it at his head while he reached for his gun. It smashed against his forehead with a loud thud and he went down, landing so hard that I heard the unmistakable sound of his head cracking against the marble floor. Almost immediately, blood began to pool out and I got stuck watching as the memories from the night CiCi died flooded my mind. My breathing became restricted, and my knees buckled beneath me. Despite him coming to kill and possibly rape me, I couldn't help being overcome with the possibility that I'd killed someone else. As I spiraled, I heard Kay Kay's little slippered feet sliding across the floor, bringing me back to reality. Breathing heavily, I scrambled to my feet and tried to beat her to the doorway. I managed to catch her just as she reached the end of the hall.

"What took so long? Who was at the door?" she questioned, trying to look past me, but I quickly turned her around and ushered her back toward the kitchen.

"Oh, it was somebody with the wrong address. I was trying to help them figure out who they were looking for," I spoke in a rush since I could already see her forehead creasing as she prepared to further question me, but I hurried and added, "You know what? I forgot I need to grab a surprise for your daddy from my brother's house. Let's go get it before he comes back." I continued walking through the kitchen and to the garage door, snatching up the keys to Heavy's BMW on the way. It was easiest to handle considering he'd been teaching me how to drive in it. I still wasn't one hundred percent confident in my driving skills but I was ready to risk it all just to get away from the dead nigga lying in the foyer.

"Wait, Adore, we still got on our pajamas," Kay Kay complained from the backseat as I slid behind the wheel.

"It's okay, we'll be right back," I lied, not knowing what else to say to explain why we were leaving in our PJ's. Judging from the look on her face, she wasn't satisfied with my answer at all but instead of arguing, she buckled herself in with a shrug.

Once we were both clicked in I pushed the start button and lifted the garage door, giving myself a pep talk before easing out into the driveway the way we'd practiced. I was barely off the block when I realized I'd left my phone, but it was too late to turn back now. Thankfully, Quay's house wasn't too far away and I didn't have to jump on the highway to get there. I breathed a sigh of relief seeing his car in the driveway and wasted no time helping Kay Kay out.

"Yo', what the fu—I mean, what the heck you doing out here like this?" Quay was already on the porch before I could make it around the car, trying to hide the gun in his hand from Kay Kay. "Where Heavy at?" He eyed me as we walked up the steps looking pissed off.

"We don't know. We came to get his surprise before he comes back though," Kay Kay spilled before I could open my mouth. I gave him a look as we passed, letting him know that something was up.

"Ohhh yeeeaah, his surprise," he dragged. "Why don't you go watch TV while we go grab it. SpongeBob is already on in there." Hearing that one of her favorite cartoons was on had her running in the direction he'd pointed. As soon as she was out of earshot, I dragged Quay in the opposite way. Immediately, I began filling him in on what was going on, making his face ball up with each revelation until I got to the part about the man that Niko's daddy sent for me.

"Hold up, that nigga did what!"

"Lower your voice!" I hissed, peeking around him to make sure Kay Kay hadn't crept our way. "He didn't do anything because I knocked him out with one of Heavy's vases, and he cracked his head on the floor, so I think he's dead."

"And you just left his ass there?" His frown deepened and I couldn't help but roll my eyes.

"What the fuck else was I supposed to do, Quay? Drag his ass into the trunk in front of Kay Kay?" Sighing, he stepped back and scrubbed his hand down his face.

"You right, my bad. I need to go get that shit taken care of before the police find a reason to come through that bitch though." He was already on his phone typing away just as Isis came around the corner with a big bowl of cereal.

"What shit, and where the police coming through? And why the hell you over here in a nightgown?" she quizzed, eyebrows drawing together as her eyes bounced between us. Clamping my mouth shut, I looked at Quay, who was just as dumbfounded as me. We'd agreed to keep all of this away from her in order to keep her stress at bay, but there was no way she was going to let this shit slide. It was all about to come out, and I just hoped I wasn't the reason that something went wrong with her pregnancy.

CHAPTER TWO
HEAVY

I paced the small cell they were housing me in and tried not to tear some shit up. Not only had I been worried sick about Adore and Kay Kay, but I also had the weight of what happened to Sha'ron on my shoulders. I had to admit, I never saw this shit coming. Sure, Black had proven to play dirty, but to involve my baby mama just to get at Adore was beyond anything I thought he was capable of. I was pissed that he'd seemingly gotten the best of me in such a ridiculous ass way, and even though I knew they couldn't hold me for long, it would still give him time to have something done to Adore, who as far as I was concerned was still in the dark about all this shit.

"Aye, it's been fuckin' hours! Give me my phone call before I tear this muhfucka up!" I yelled in frustration to no one in particular. I'd seen at least ten officers just leisurely walking around and not one had come through to let me make a call, and I was livid. Finally, a busty ass female officer strolled over with a smirk on her face that I wanted to slap off.

"Mr. Stone, yelling and throwing a tantrum is not going to

get you anywhere in here." She poked her chest out even further and leaned up against the bars, licking her thin ass lips. "I might be able to help you out if you promise to give me a call once you're released." As bad as I wanted to tell her to run her ass in the middle of the Dan Ryan Expressway, I forced a cocky grin, even though I was sure it looked more like a grimace.

"Shiiiit, you let me use the phone and I'll do you one better and meet you at your car after your shift," I lied. There was no way I had any intention on fucking with her thirsty ass, but she flashed every tooth in her mouth and damn near broke her neck to unlock my cell.

"Come on before somebody comes this way."

I wasted no time stepping out and waiting as she locked the now empty cell back before slipping her arm through mine like she was afraid I'd run off. I was thankful that the phone was only around a corner, because I was ready for her to get her crusty ass hands off me. As soon as I stopped in front of the phone, I shook her off me, but that didn't stop her from standing close by breathing down my neck. The first person I called was my lawyer and let him know to get his ass down to the station ASAP. After confirming he was on his way, I hung up and immediately dialed up Adore, hanging up after getting her voicemail. I could feel shorty eyeing me hard, but that didn't stop me from calling her again and this time leaving a message for her to go to Quay's house as soon as she got the message.

"Hey—" The look I gave stopped whatever protest she was about to make as I dialed my mama's number next.

"He-hello?" Hearing my OG's voice caused me to sigh in relief.

"Hey Ma—"

"Oh my god, Dominique! Are you okay? I saw what happened and I know damn well you didn't do nothin' like that! I been up to the police station and they won't tell me nothin'! I swear to God I'm gone sue the dog shit out they asses! By the time I'm done, yo' name gone be on this muhfuckin' building, and I put that on my—"

"Wait, you up here right now?" I quizzed, looking around like I'd be able to see her. She was going off so much that I could hardly keep up, but I caught the part where she said *this* building real quick.

"Yeah, I'm still waiting for one of these assholes to give me some information!" Her voice raised like she was talking directly to one of the officers, and I shook my head. My mama was usually calm cool and collected until you fucked with somebody in her family. I rarely ever heard her ass curse so much, so I knew she was beyond pissed and was giving them hell in the front of the police station.

"Ayite, well don't get locked up tryna cuss them muhfuckas out. My lawyer already on the way, just hold tight. Did you drop by the crib this morning though?" I needed to know, holding my breath as I awaited her answer.

"Tuh! I wish the fuck they would try and put me in cuffs." She sucked her teeth but lowered her damn voice like I knew she would. "Anyway, I stopped through there before I came here and let her know what was going on; well, that you were locked up anyway. I told her I was on my way here though to find out what I could."

Immediately I was concerned about why the fuck if she knew I was in jail would she not answer the phone. As bad as I wanted to press her to see what type of mood Adore was in when she told her what happened, I knew I didn't have enough time. Officer airbag titties was behind me huffing and puffing like the big bad wolf and clearing her throat repeatedly, letting me know I was running low on time. It was cool though, because as soon as my lawyer Perry arrived, I was going to be released fast as fuck. He was a beast when it came to this law shit and regardless of what Black's crooked ass had done, I was sure he'd have them all shaking in their boots by the time he was done.

"Ayite, I gotta go. I been holdin' up the line for a minute. I'ma talk to you soon."

"Okay, I'm gone be up here waiting 'cause I'm not leavin' till they let you out," she huffed, hanging up before I could say anything back. Shaking my head, I went ahead and placed the phone back on the hook, ignoring the attitude old girl clearly had. Still huffing, she sidled up next to me, wrapping her arm back around mine.

"You better make it worth my while later. We almost just got caught a couple times." Rolling her eyes, she stopped to unlock my cell, careful to check and make sure nobody was coming. At this point I no longer cared about her feelings since I'd gotten what I wanted already. Low key, she was dumb to agree to that shit before I held up my end of the bargain, but that was her fault for being a goofy.

"Don't even worry about that. You need to be more worried about the sexual harassment suit I'ma hit yo' ass with once I get out this bitch!" I frowned down at her in disgust as I slid back into the cell. Her mouth opened and closed as she tried to gather herself. "Get yo' dumbass up out my face before I call your superior right now and let them know they got a freak back here tryna offer her dusty pussy to niggas that's locked up."

Too stunned to speak, she hurriedly locked me back in and scampered off, leaving me alone. Once she was out of sight I went to sit on the hard ass bench, resting my head back on the wall and closing my eyes. I'd been up for hours dealing with this bullshit and besides being tired, I was overcome with worry.

I didn't know how much time had passed when I was awakened by an officer screaming my name like a fool. If it wasn't for the sound of keys jingling I would've ignored dude's rude ass, but sensing that Perry had come through, I hopped right up. Just like I'd thought, Perry stood off to the side giving the cop a nasty look.

"You're already in hot water Simpson, don't make it worse," he warned, causing the person I now knew as Simpson to snort irritably. His ass knew not to say shit else though, as he ushered me out of the cell and locked it back. "You'll be hearing from me." Having thoroughly shaken the man up, Perry allowed me to walk ahead of him before following me down the hallway.

"About damn time!" My OG was the first face I saw coming from the back and she rushed over, hugging me to her before pulling back slightly. Grumbling, she checked me for any visible signs of injury.

"Ma, man chill, I'm good." I chuckled, slipping my arm around her so we could leave as Perry filled me in on what was going on. I couldn't even deny the relief I felt hearing that Sha'ron was alive but in critical condition. Despite my ill feelings toward her, I never wanted any harm to come her way on account of me, and fucking around with Black's bitch ass, that's exactly what happened. I hated that I even shared the same DNA as that nigga and I tried hard to forget that shit, which was why he'd made it a point to mention it when he'd popped up at the police station. I'd only found out the day of my high school graduation when he decided to drop by and talk to my mama about me. He thought he'd be able to just slip in like he'd always done and run her some money, but he got the shock of his life when I came to the door behind her. His ass looked like he'd seen a ghost while my OG just seemed irritated. Instead of explaining it away, she went ahead and let me know that he was my father. I had to admit, at the time I didn't know how to feel. By then I was basically a grown ass man myself and the last thing I needed was a nigga trying to play daddy to me. Apparently, he wasn't interested in that shit either since he already had his golden boy, De'Niko, following closely in his footsteps. All he'd been trying to do was hand off some money like he'd been doing since I was born and proven to be his actual son. He felt like being there financially absolved him of his duties, and I was sure it helped him sleep better at night after basically trying to turn my mama into a mistress. Once I found out about it though, I insisted she keep whatever he gave her and spend it on herself because I didn't want shit from him. At least that's what I was thinking at the time. Once his ass became the mayor though, I realized I could actually use him for something, unbeknownst to my OG. Real shit, she was going to go the fuck off on my ass when she found out I was connected to that nigga and that he was the one behind all this. I was hoping I'd be able to keep it from her though.

"Alright, try to stay out of trouble for the time being. We got them by the balls right now with the shit they pulled, but I don't wanna give them any ammunition to come fucking with you," Perry advised, shaking my hand firmly.

"I got you," I managed to lie with ease. Behind my shorty and my baby mama, I was about to bring all the smoke, but he didn't need to know that. Smiling, he said his goodbyes and headed to his car while we went in the opposite direction. By now I was damn near dragging my mama down the street, trying to rush back to Adore and my baby. Something still wasn't sitting right with me about her not answering the phone and I quickly tried again to call her, only to receive her voicemail again. That only had me moving faster as my OG complained behind me.

"Boy, I know you better stop dragging me down this street like a rag doll! I know if you make my old ass fall, it's gone be me and you!" she snapped, finally snatching away once we came upon her gold Lexus. Breathing heavily, she gave me an evil glare before digging through her huge ass purse.

"My bad, but let me drive, Ma. I need to make sure Adore and Kay Kay are okay. It's been hours and I ain't heard from either of them. I ain't tryna take all day getting there." She didn't seem happy about handing her keys over but she didn't put up a fuss like I expected her to. Hitting the key fob, I opened the passenger door for her before going around to the driver's side. I couldn't even get in myself until I adjusted her seat since she had it all the way up, but it was still a tight fit. My mama just looked at me smugly as I pulled off into traffic. Despite the uncomfortable drive, or maybe because of it, I made it home in record time.

Seeing Quay's truck in my driveway put me on high alert, and I barely put the car in park before hopping out and telling my mama to stay put. I couldn't help but think the worst, especially when I got through the front door and saw them wrapping a nigga up in my expensive ass Persian rug.

"What the fuck happened in here? Where Adore and Kay Kay?" I panicked, taking in the scene. One of my heavy ass vases was on its side in the corner and a big puddle of blood was running from the body to underneath the hall table.

"They're both good, they at my crib with Ice. Apparently, this nigga just knocked on the door and upped a pistol on Adore ass. She fucked his ass up with that vase though." Quay nodded to the vase with a chuckle and his boy joined in. I real life wanted to kick my own ass for not preparing her for the off chance that somebody could penetrate the bubble I'd created. If she hadn't thought quick on her feet, I could've walked in on her and my baby's bodies. I silently thanked the man upstairs for looking out for them when I couldn't, before taking a peek at the nigga in the carpet. He was a local hitta that only a few niggas actually used because he was unprofessional as fuck. How Black had gotten ahold of him was beyond me, but I didn't have any time to speculate on that. I needed to get to my girl and my baby, so after covering him back up I sent a message to my cleanup crew so they could come dispose of his ass properly.

CHAPTER THREE
QUAY

Seeing how Heavy's cleanup crew showed up and scrubbed the scene had me feeling like I was on an episode of *CSI* or some shit. Them niggas came through with whole hazmat suits and got straight to work. Despite it not appearing to be a messy ass scene, they flipped on the blue light and showed blood and DNA in places I would've never thought to look. I stood in awe watching them work like it was a movie or something, all my ass needed was some popcorn. I could tell Rock was just as impressed, even though he was trying to act like it wasn't a big deal since he was still salty about his last encounter with Heavy. Even when we'd pulled up, his damn jaw almost hit the floor just seeing the outside of Heavy's mansion. I had to admit the big homie was living large, and I couldn't wait to put my family up in something just as nice.

Before I knew it an hour had passed and they were leaving the same way they'd entered. After getting rid of his OG, Heavy had stuck around and watched them for a few before heading upstairs to shower. I checked my watch when he still hadn't come back down once they'd left, and slouched down in my seat as Rock sucked his teeth like a bitch.

"Man, what's taking his ass so long? We still got shit to do!" he finally huffed, breaking the silence in the room. I side eyed his ass immediately because he knew he didn't have shit going on.

"Nigga, you ain't tryna do shit but run up behind Tanya's ass." I chuckled, talking about his on again-off again girlfriend. The only reason he was even so pressed was because he'd found out she was fucking with another nigga. I couldn't front, I'd have been on the same shit with Ice. I was still tight about her fucking around with Heavy's right hand, but for the sake of my baby I was putting that shit to the side. His face balled up into a deep frown and he was already shaking his head in denial.

"Ain't nobody thinkin' 'bout shorty! I already got something else lined up. Fuck Tanya!"

Shaking my head, I didn't even try to hide my laughter. "Yeah, ayite nigga, keep tellin' yourself that!" I didn't have any type of advice for his ass since I was dealing with my own shit, but I could tell a sick in love nigga when I saw one. Without any type of argument, he waved me off, grumbling just as Heavy entered the room.

"My bad, I had a couple calls to make," he explained, looking up from his phone briefly.

"It's cool, you can follow me back to the crib, 'cause Ice blowing up my phone and I know Adore the one got her doin' that shit." Scoffing, I stood up, straightening out my clothes, and Rock followed suit. "We gone need to figure out something else to keep her ass safe though, 'cause them muhfuckas getting too bold." I'd been trying to keep my cool about the situation because Adore had come out unscathed, besides being shook the fuck up. My sister wasn't the type to hurt a fly and had somehow ended up catching a whole body because of her dumb ass baby daddy and his people. At this point I felt like the only option was to go ahead and kill De'Niko Sr. I knew for sure once he was out of the picture his son wouldn't be on shit because he was too scary to move on his own.

"I'm already working on it. I know you ready to blow that nigga brains out, shit I'm on that same shit," he said like he was reading my mind. "With Adore in a court case with him though, it would look bad for her. We gotta move smarter than that, because if anything happens to them, even if it looks like an accident, they gone scrutinize that shit hard as hell." I could understand where he was coming from, but I didn't really want to hear that shit. The Black family had been getting away with shit for years. My sister had lost eight years of her life fucking with them and there was no telling what other things they'd done. I fucked with Heavy tough, but I couldn't say I was confident in his ability to get this one handled. He was too calculated, too careful, and while that may have benefited him in the drug game, I wasn't sure it would help us any when it came to the likes of the Black family.

"I hear you bro, but he already making moves that's putting my family at risk and yours too. We can't just let his ass get away with this shit. That's how Adore ended up going to prison and then signing that bullshit ass contract, because he never got any consequences for his actions. He ain't doin' shit but getting more and more bold every time I turn around, and we're the only ones taking losses." I kept my tone even, although I was heated on the inside as Heavy blew out a deep breath.

"I feel you, I do, but I ain't tryna misstep and have Adore going down for some shit we did. You already know with her background they'll be happy to pin that shit on her no matter how obvious it is that she ain't do it. You willing to risk her freedom for his ass? I mean, yeah, he'll be dead, but you'll still be without a sister and y'all damn sure won't have Kaliyah back." He was right. I knew he was, just like always, I just hated to admit it. Shit had me wishing Adore never got involved with that nigga in the first place, but I quickly erased the thought since that would mean my niece wouldn't exist.

"You right," I finally admitted with a sigh. He eyed me for a minute like he was studying me before relief washed over his face and he gave a stiff nod.

"Ayite, I know it seems like this shit movin' too slow for you, but trust me when I say I'm not playin' when it comes to yo' sister. I'ma make sure that nigga get his though, I just can't make that shit happen overnight." Sighing, I slapped hands with him in a silent agreement. I could feel Rock's ass burning a hole in the side of my face and knew it was in disbelief. This was the second time he'd seen me be on some chill shit, which was definitely not like me. I was more laid back than Manny was, but it wasn't typical for me to seemingly just back down from some shit I didn't agree with. If he didn't understand everything Heavy had just laid out and why it made sense to agree, then he was dumb as hell.

"Bro, you really going along with that bullshit dude was talkin'?" he quizzed as soon as we were in my whip alone, and I blew out a frustrated breath. I should've known he wasn't gone let that shit slide, but I figured he'd at least wait a little bit before calling me out.

"I'm goin' along with whatever keeps my sister out of prison. You willin' to go instead or you just givin' out unnecessary opinions?" My eyes darted between him and the road and just like I thought, his ass began stuttering.

"I-I ain't sayin' for me to do shit. I just mean we could pay somebody just like his ass did. Somebody willing to take the fall if shit get hot. It's plenty niggas around the hood that would be ready to do a bid for Heavy's ass. You ain't even thought of no alternatives before you just took his word for it that—"

The look I sent his way silenced him immediately, as it should have. One thing I hated for sure was somebody questioning me, and he knew that. Throwing his hands up, he started to backtrack but I cut his ass off. "Aye, why don't you just shut the fuck up talkin' to me before you say something else you gone regret!"

"Ayite man, damn," he grumbled, turning his attention out the window. I was thankful he kept that same energy for the rest of the ride, getting right out and climbing into his own car. Unmoved by his little tantrum, I led Heavy inside and was damn near knocked down when Adore and Kay Kay saw his ass behind me. I hurried and got the fuck out the way, while Isis watched them with a big smile.

"This the second time yo' ass done been outta bed, ain't it? I know you ain't been down here this whole time." I grimaced and her face instantly fell.

"Considering the situation, I didn't think it'd be an issue to sit down here with my *best friend*. It ain't like I been able to see her since y'all been keeping her safe." Rolling her eyes, she used air quotes for that last part trying to be funny. I could tell that us keeping her in the dark about Adore had hurt her feelings, but if she thought she was gonna get an apology or something then she was crazy. I wasn't at all sorry for trying to protect my baby, and if it wasn't absolutely necessary then she still wouldn't have found out if I had anything to do with it. The look I gave after her dramatics had her sucking her teeth loudly as she prepared to take her ass back to bed. Since she'd been on her feet too many times already, I pulled my pants up higher on my waist and scooped her up bridal style. She knew better than to try and fight me but judging from how tight her lips got, I knew she was pissed. It seemed like I was making everybody get in their feelings today, but oh fucking well.

I carried her up to her room with ease and set her ass right in the bed. She snatched away when I tried to help her get under the covers, and I laughed at her childish ass. "Can you at least send Adore up to say goodbye since you cut our visit short, *father*?" she sassed, not even looking at me as she reached for the remote and cut on the TV. Right away the sounds of *Martin* filled the room. I watched her for a few seconds before nodding like her ass was paying me any attention.

"I got you, smart ass girl. I'm probably gone ride out with them to make sure they're good but I'll be back soon." I hid my irritation behind a chuckle as she mocked me with her face frowned up. Her attitude had been fucked up for a minute and I assumed it was because of the strict diet she was on plus having to stay in bed, but I didn't have time to try to fuck it up out of her at the moment. Isis wasn't nowhere near as tough with my dick in her. I couldn't lie, with as much shit as I had on my shoulders, I needed a release too, but I'd save that for later.

By the time I made it back downstairs only Heavy was in the living room. He was on the phone cursing somebody out, but he quickly hung up upon me entering the room. "Where everybody go?"

"They went to go change their clothes real quick before we leave, but I might need you to take them to the new spot. I can't find John and I'm gone have to run up to the hospital. Them muhfuckas not tryna give me no info on my baby mama." I could see the frustration on his face. No doubt he was going through it considering the shit going on with my sister, the disappearance of his most loyal soldier, and his baby mama. All of that was enough to make any man stressed.

"Ayite, I can do that, but who you gone have keep an eye on

them while you're gone?" I just had to ask. As shook up as my sister was after everything that happened this morning, it wasn't no way she'd be comfortable alone at an undisclosed location.

"I got a few workers, plus Hector volunteered a few of his people if I needed them to—"

"You trust that muhfucka with my sister and yo' shorty?"

"Hector ain't got no reason to cross me, especially after getting paid just to play middle man and at this point, he's all I got. I can't put a freeze on production to wait this out, or else I'll be owing his ass even more money." He must have noticed my unease with that plan because he quickly followed up with, "Just bear with me, ayite. We just need to get Adore to court and see how this plays out." His phone going off snatched his attention before I could speak. He wasted no time answering it and ending our conversation in the process. I couldn't lie, as much as I trusted his input, I felt like between his mans missing and the random nigga showing up at his door there was some other shit going on. However, if worse came to worse, I'd be packing up and going to watch my sister's back myself.

CHAPTER FOUR

ISIS

I was anxious as fuck after finding out everything that was going on with Adore, and I was pissed that Quay had banished me to my bedroom like I shouldn't be a part of the conversation. Those two factors alone had me sitting in bed stewing hours after they'd all finally left. At least he had kept his promise and sent my girl upstairs to say goodbye, but I was still salty as fuck and not even *Martin* reruns or my secret stash of snacks were helping my mood. The sound of somebody entering the house had me scrambling to put away the Oreos I'd been eating and shortly after, Ms. Deb was peeking her head in my door. Irritated that it wasn't Quay, I rolled my eyes inwardly. It was nothing against Ma, but I knew she was only there to babysit me, because she never came in the house so early.

"Nuh uh, don't be lookin' at me like that, lil' girl," she joked sassily, coming all the way inside and sitting on the edge of my bed. Despite my attitude, I couldn't help the smile that tugged at my lips as she grabbed my big toe playfully.

"I wasn't making a face, I had heartburn." The lie rolled off my tongue and she looked at me doubtfully.

"First of all, ain't no heart burn got you lookin' like that. I know what it looks like when a muhfucka is disappointed to see me."

"I'm sorry, it's not that I'm disappointed. I just feel like I'm the only one stuck here in this bed while Quay gets to come and go as he pleases. Earlier he carried me up here to bed just to leave again." Out loud it sounded like a childish issue, but I wasn't taking it back. I was already tired of being stuck in the house and I still had months to go. Her expression grew serious and she shifted on the bed so she was almost completely facing me.

"Well, it seems like you're taking this the wrong way. You're thinking this is some type of punishment, but it's really your first assignment as a mama. It may not seem like it, but staying in bed and resting is important, and even though it may suck, just think about how great it's going to be when you finally get to hold your healthy baby. As far as Quay goes, he's dealing with a lot right now, but he's trying. Remember, he's going through this with you and if you feel like he's not doing his part then you need to let him know. Having an attitude and giving him the silent treatment ain't gone cut it." I hated to admit it, but she was right. Besides fucking, I really wasn't talking to Quay unless I needed something or to snap at him because of how frustrated I was. I hadn't even mentioned him taking me to my store since he'd canceled on me the last time. When I thought about it, it didn't make sense to be walking around with an attitude about something that may have slipped his mind with everything else he was taking care of. Feeling bad, I released a sigh.

"You're right," I agreed with a nod. "I guess I could try a little harder." Smiling, she gave my leg a squeeze.

"Good. Now all you gotta do is stop eating shit you not supposed to and you'll be good. I'm gone let you slide this time, but if I catch you again I'm snitchin'." She raised a brow as I frowned in confusion. I wasn't about to admit that I wasn't following my diet but how she knew that was beyond me.

"Huh?"

"Girl, don't huh me. You got crumbs all over your shirt and I don't know any fruits or vegetables that leave those." My head immediately dropped to my baby blue shirt that showed evidence of the Oreos I'd been eating just before she came in there. "Mmhmm," she said, giving me a knowing look as she strolled back out. Sucking my teeth, I hurried to brush my shirt and blanket clean even though I was already caught.

I'd really taken our conversation to heart, but that didn't stop me from getting dressed to go to my shop the next day as soon as she left for work. Snacks I could probably do without, but after having my mama in my ear, there was no way I could go without my own income. In my opinion it was much less dangerous to go to work since I'd be sitting the whole time. As soon as I stepped inside I cut on the lights and adjusted the heat before switching to my seat behind the counter. Talking to Deb had given me the idea to hire somebody to move my inventory, then I could get set up at home and start working on a website. I'd been spending a lot of time being sneaky and irritated, but my time at home would probably be more pleasant if I occupied my time with more constructive things.

In between helping customers, I made a few calls to local movers to see if I could schedule somebody to come out. It took no time to book with Moving Bros and after penciling them in for the next day, I stuck around for a couple more hours. I was about to lock up when someone rushed into the door. The last person I was expecting to see when they flipped back their hood was my mama, looking as if she'd just gotten off a shift from the bank she worked at.

"God damn, it's cold out there!" she fussed, wrapping her arms around herself for extra warmth. Unsure of what she was doing here, I eyed her quizzically before giving a dry greeting.

"Hey Ma." My tone stopped her from looking around and she set her hard glare on me.

"*Hey Ma?* Don't sound so excited to see me. It ain't like I'm the one that hung up the phone on you the last time we talked and ain't answered my phone since," she immediately went in, and I rolled my eyes and began walking back to my seat with her following closely behind.

"I'm actually on bedrest Ma, so if all you're going to do is try to stress me out then you can go ahead and leave," I huffed, sinking down into my swivel chair and rolling my eyes. Just because her cruel words had pushed me to work even harder didn't mean I wanted her around me. Her eyes bucked at my rudeness since I hadn't ever really talked to her like that, but obviously being around Quay had my tongue even more lethal than usual.

"Well, if you're on bedrest then you shouldn't be at work, but we all know that's how shit is when you're pregnant by an ain't shit nigga. It ain't my fault you're delusional!" Just from the satisfied grin on her face I could tell she was pleased with herself, and I couldn't do shit but shake my head. I'd heard about women who were jealous of their daughters or who tried to make their daughters' lives hell. My mama was definitely the latter, but at this point I didn't even know if I could blame her for the reason why.

"I don't *have to* work, Ma. If you must know, Quay takes very good care of us. I'm far from delusional." I put emphasis on what I was saying and rubbed my growing belly. "I'm here because I'm bored being stuck in bed. You know I'm not the type to sit around not doing nothing with myself." It felt like I was throwing my life up in her face and to an extent, I was. My mama had allowed my father to make her bitter about life in general. I can't front, she took very good care of me, sometimes working two or three jobs at a time to do so, but she wasn't happy about it. I'd learned a long time ago that my care was really a slap in the face of my deadbeat. She wanted him to know that she was doing just fine without him and didn't need a man, despite how unhappy it made her to overwork herself. She tried to instill those same things into me and for a while I had drank the Kool-Aid, feeling as if I didn't want or need a man to do shit for me. I quickly learned that was a crazy way to think. No, I didn't *need* a man, but having one around that could help carry the load was amazing. There were a lot of things I held issue with when it came to Quay, but him having my back and helping me wasn't one of them.

My little speech only had her turning up her nose though, either choosing not to believe or simply not wanting to hear it. "Isis please, all niggas behave in the beginning and then as soon as you get too far along to do anything about it, that's when they show their ass. I guess I should be happy that you're at least still making your own money so you're not all the way dick dizzy."

"Oooookay, again Mama, what did you stop by for? I was just about to close." I sighed, just wanting her to say her peace and leave at this point. Her eyes flittered around like she was looking for something else to talk shit about before landing back on me when she came up empty.

"I was actually just coming to check on you since you haven't been answering my calls, but everything seems to be okay I guess." I resisted the urge to roll my eyes at how unhappy she seemed to be about me being okay, in her words. She'd literally been in my store for all of ten minutes and hadn't said shit nice or asked about my baby, and I was grateful that Quay had encouraged me to cut her off for the time being. I could only hope that she got her shit together by the time I delivered, or else I was going to have to consider whether or not I wanted her around my baby with her negative ass talking points.

"Well, thanks for stopping by Ma. I'll try to do better about keeping in touch, but I really need to be getting home soon," I spoke fast as I damn near pushed her back out the door. When she finally left and pulled off, I cut off the open sign and shut everything down so I could go home and take a nap. Dealing with her had definitely drained the hell out of me.

CHAPTER FIVE

DE'NIKO JR

I stood in court trying to keep my anger in check as the judge looked at me and my family in disgust. My parents were sitting right behind me along with Farrah, and I could almost feel the heat radiating off my dad. I looked over at Adore, who had her eyes locked on the judge as her mom and Heavy sat behind her. She looked so good that I could hardly stop staring at her, even though her lawyer was handing mine his ass.

"Your Honor, I'd like to have this agreement thrown out considering that my client was underage as well as under duress since she was pregnant at the time. The Black family used their influence and money to convince a child without legal representation to sign over the rights to her child with impossible stipulations for her to be able to get her child back—"

"That's not true!" my dad hopped up shouting, and the judge immediately set her steely gaze on him.

"Mr. Black, I advise you to have a seat and not interrupt these proceedings again, or else I will have you removed or held in contempt." She barely raised her voice but it was obvious she meant business.

"Sit down, De'Niko!" my mother hissed as my lawyer tried to urge him into silence, but he simply refused. Even I had to turn around and say something, because the last thing we needed was the press to find out he was arrested or kicked out of the courtroom.

"No, this is ridiculous! That woman is a murderer and was in prison when I decided to help her out by taking in her child! I refuse to sit here and be insulted and made out to be the bad guy! I'm the mayor for Christ's sake!"

"That's it Mr. Black! Bailiff, please escort the *mayor* from my courtroom!" I immediately closed my eyes with a sigh, seeing just how bad this had gone. Everyone was silent as my father was led out of the courtroom screaming, and as soon as the doors opened I could hear the reporters asking questions and trying to take pictures of this mess. "Now I'd like for the remainder of this hearing to go on without any more outbursts, is that clear, Mr. Walker?" the judge asked my attorney, who quickly agreed, giving me and the rest of my family a warning look. I was sure that my mother would never act out the way my father had. She was always completely in control, and for the most part Farrah was a mini version of her, so I was sure we wouldn't have any more issues.

"As I was saying, this entire agreement should be discarded considering the reasons I previously stated in addition to my client being involved in an inappropriate relationship with the defendant. At the time of their relationship Adore was only seventeen years old while Mr. Black was well into his twenties, giving him a clear emotional and mental advantage over her."

"It does appear that there were many odds stacked against your client; however, like the mayor stated, Adore was arrested for the murder of another young lady during this time," Judge

Howard said, and I instantly grew tense. I hated talking about CiCi. After all of these years I'd never had to explain anything pertaining to her. No one questioned me about it and it was just another dirty little secret that my name had managed to sweep under the rug. Smartly, I kept my eyes straight ahead because I knew that Farrah was probably shooting daggers my way. CiCi was just another reminder of my infidelities.

"Your Honor, I'd like to mention that the victim was also an underaged girl that was brainwashed by the defendant. Although tragic, her death was an accident that happened when my pregnant and scared client tried to defend herself against an attack. The fact that the person she trusted the most left her open to attack while she was carrying his child and then subjected her to prison is even more of a reason to question his moral compass."

"Hey, say something! She's over there tearing me apart!" I leaned over and whispered to my lawyer. He was being way too relaxed about this whole thing and I was beginning to think I should've defended myself. Clearing his throat, he finally stood up, causing all eyes to fall on him.

"I object, Your Honor, none of this has anything to do with why we're here today. My client may have done some things he wasn't proud of in his younger years, but he's a respected member of society with a family now and whether or not he made mistakes, he's the one that has been constant in the minor's life so far when her mother was behind bars for recklessly killing another girl because of her own jealousy." I couldn't help grinning inwardly and rejoicing at the comeback he'd made, despite it not being true. Everyone on Adore's side looked pissed off down to her lawyer, but she had to know we'd fight dirty if need be. She'd be lucky if I didn't have him mention how close she seemed to Heavy, who I knew had ties to the street. Sure, I negotiated deals between him and my father, but being the type of street nigga he was, I knew he'd never snitch even to the detriment of himself, which could come in handy at a later date if he continued to stick his nose in our business.

"Well, regardless of the circumstances, Ms. Wallace has paid her debt to society and I have to admit that the terms of this contract are problematic, so I will not uphold them at this time. However, Ms. Wallace, considering your background and the fact that the minor in question has no knowledge of you, besides what she's learned just recently, I will grant you supervised visits effective immediately, until you become better acquainted, at which time I will take into consideration your progress and the child's feelings. Court adjourned, Clerk, please give us a date for three months from now." My mouth fell open as she banged her gavel and stood, exiting the courtroom while Adore and her family squealed and hugged excitedly. I could hear Farrah forcing out tears behind me as my mother talked shit under her breath, and I was glued to my seat in disbelief. I couldn't even hear whatever the fuck it was that my lawyer was saying to me over the sound of my own thoughts. This shit was highly unexpected. Everything always went in our favor, but I should've known something was going to go wrong when the judge we wanted couldn't take the case. I finally stood up from my seat with my fists balled up angrily. I was mad enough to actually punch someone and I might've used my lawyer as an outlet as soon as we were away from the public eye.

"You won't get away with this, I can promise you that, you little menace! There's no way I'm going to lose my only grandchild to the likes of you!" My mother's voice snatched me out of my thoughts as she threatened Adore.

"Girl, go to hell!" Adore's mom shouted back, prompting her to clutch her pearls before switching out of the courtroom.

With pursed lips, I reached for Farrah's hand so we could walk out a united front, but she snatched away and went running behind my mom, leaving only me and my lawyer with Adore's family. She was crying and hugging her mom, not paying me any attention, but Heavy's eyes were zeroed in on me. Despite the smile on his face, I could tell it was nothing but malice there and I couldn't deny being shook up. I wasted no time hightailing it out of there, much more frightened of him than I was of the paparazzi. Our security team met me at the door and tried their hardest to shield me from the many flashing cameras and microphones being shoved in my face. I managed to make it to the awaiting car where my father was silently stewing. My mother just kept shifting in her seat and clearing her throat or sighing, while Farrah stared out of the window with dried tears all over her face. I immediately felt like I was the target of everyone's anger, and that point was further proven when my Sr. brought his hand up and slapped the shit out of me upon closing the door. Biting back the pain I felt, my mouth tightened into a straight line, knowing that showing any sign of emotion would only set him off further.

"This is your fault! Not only did you get involved with that trash, but you impregnated her! After everything I've done to protect this family, your actions are constantly doing the exact opposite! I swear, if you weren't my son I'd wash my fucking hands of you!"

"Oh shut it, De'Niko! This is just as much your fault as it is his! Where do you think he gets his appetite for young ghetto women?" My head snapped in my mother's direction at the implication. As far as I knew, my father had never so much as looked at another woman. I'd never heard them even arguing about infidelities, so this was news to me. Even Farrah was now done with her fake pity party and completely engrossed in the conversation.

"Let's not act like I'm the only one he could've gotten it from! You want to talk about ghetto, how about having to write up endless NDAs because you can't keep your hands off the staff!" my father spewed, leaning forward and pointing a finger in her face.

Gasping, my mother clutched her chest before quickly recovering and narrowing her eyes on him. "Well, maybe if you had thought of NDAs a long time ago, you wouldn't have an illegitimate so—"

"You shut your fucking mouth!"

"Woah! Hey!" I shouted, finally intervening when it looked like my father was about to attack her. I was completely stunned and so was my mother, who was frozen in fear. A heavy silence fell over the car as I moved in between them and tried to make sense of everything that had just been said. It was a lot to take in and much more than I cared to hear, but I couldn't shake the curiosity of what my mother was about to say before he tried to attack her. Swallowing hard, I tried to fix my lips to further question him, but it was proving difficult. "D-Dad, what is she talking about?" I stammered, looking at him timidly. There was no way he'd fathered someone else and never mentioned it or brought them around, not after he'd made such a big deal about us taking in Kaliyah.

"Go ahead and tell him, De'Niko. Tell our son how when he was a little boy, you went out and got some guttersnipe pregnant and allowed her to have that bastard!" My mom's lips trembled as she spoke, throwing me for a loop even more. Gloria Black never showed emotion, and she definitely didn't cry, so to see her so worked up let me know that she was at her wit's end. Turning back to Sr., I was praying he'd deny this, that he'd reassure me that there was some type of mistake, but the hateful glare he was sending her way told me everything I needed to know. Like a coward, he couldn't even look at me, and for some reason I chuckled uncomfortably.

"Is this shit true, I have a brother somewhere? Do you know who he is?" I shifted, growing angry myself. His jaw clenched and he glanced my way after a few seconds.

"*Yes*," he grit, obviously not happy about having to say, but he should've known that I would want every detail when it came to a long-lost sibling. Raising a brow, I leaned even closer, encouraging him to continue. "It's Dominique, alright! Are you happy now? Heavy is your brother!" I swear it felt like he'd knocked the fucking wind out of me and I hated that I'd even asked. The day had truly taken a turn for the worst, and after everything that happened I'd likely not ever be able to recover.

CHAPTER SIX

ADORE

I was still riding on cloud nine several days after my win in court. The judge had granted me two hours every Saturday for the first month and it would gradually go up each month after. As the weekend approached, I grew more and more excited, trying to come up with fun things we could do together. Between Kay Kay giving me tips and my damn Google searching, I already had enough activities to fill up a year's worth of time. Our first visit was only two days away and as excited as I was, I couldn't help being a little nervous. Although I'd met Kaliyah before, the circumstances were strained. She hadn't seemed afraid of me at the time, but that definitely wasn't how I'd planned our first meeting to be. I hoped I'd be able to make better memories with her, as long as the Blacks hadn't turned her against me.

"Aye, you ready to go?" Heavy eased in behind me, resting his face in the crook of my neck. The mixture of the lakefront view and his arms wrapped around me felt amazing and I started to tell him no. It would be my first day back at work since Niko had put the hit out on me and after spending so much time with Heavy, I knew I'd be having withdrawals.

"Ummm, I'm really considering playing hooky to be honest," I confessed, snuggling deeper into his body, causing him to chuckle.

"Not the way you been talkin' 'bout how you can't wait to get back to work," he stopped kissing my neck long enough to say. It was true, I had missed work and I absolutely missed making money, even though he was constantly handing me wads of cash. "Besides, my mama expecting you and I ain't tryna have her blaming me for your ass reneging. Now hurry up so I can drop yo' fine ass off." Giving me one last kiss, he tapped me on the butt before slipping away to answer his ringing phone. I instantly felt the cold from the separation, but I wasn't trying to be late anyways. The other waitresses already were probably feeling some type of way about the time I'd taken off in addition to me snagging Heavy. I didn't need to give them any more of a reason to hate me. While he finished up his call I ran to get dressed.

We'd been staying in his lakefront condo because I wasn't comfortable going back to his house after what happened there. The location made me feel safer too, being that it was in a luxury building with a doorman, so the chances of somebody just slipping up to our door were unlikely. Heavy had assured me that with the publicity of our case, Niko's daddy would have no choice but to back off. Since court they'd definitely been on the news and gossip sites every day and they'd damn sure look at them if anything happened to me. Then again, as mad as he was in court he'd probably be willing to still try, but that was what I had Heavy and a security detail for.

After handling my hygiene, I slipped on my uniform shirt, some black skinny jeans, and matching black Vapormax. My hair was beginning to revert to its curly state, so I just brushed it up into a high bun. I freshened up my baby hairs and by the time I was done, Heavy was entering the bedroom.

"I'm ready," I told him, spraying on perfume and giving myself a onceover in the mirror. I immediately blushed seeing him watching me from the doorway. "Whaaat?" Caught, he shook his head and tried to fight a smile that still broke through.

"Nothin'." He shrugged. "I just like watching you exist and being in your space." I swear it seemed like everything that came out of his mouth was poetry, and my cheeks grew even hotter as I turned around to face him.

"I like being around you too," I cooed, and before I knew it he was right in front of me enveloping me in his arms.

"Good, 'cause we're definitely locked in." My heart fluttered as he kissed me softly, and I wiggled away before it went too far. By now I only had about a half hour to get to work and I wasn't playing about being late.

I made it through the door of the restaurant just in time and I could immediately feel all eyes on me. It may have been because I was just coming back or because of the beefy ass giant that was trailing me, but my guess was that it was both. I went to the back where the kitchen was bustling and slipped on my apron.

"Hey, uh Rex, you can either have a seat back here in the office or at the bar if you'd like," I offered, and he said a gruff okay and headed back out to where the bar was. In the short amount of time he'd been trailing me, I'd learned he was a man of few words, so I wasn't even offended with his shortness. Just as he disappeared Ms. Pam came out of her office with a huge grin.

"Adore! I'm glad to see you, girl. I thought for sure you weren't gonna come today." She pulled me in for a quick embrace, making me feel good about my decision to actually come in.

"I almost didn't, but I've missed this place. Plus, I'm gone need all the money I can get since they granted me visitation." I cheesed, unable to hide my excitement.

"Oh yeah, congratulations! You deserve all the good fortune you've been getting honey and don't you let nobody tell you different." My soft ass instantly got emotional from her words of encouragement. She gave me a quick kiss on the cheek and was off at the sound of someone calling her name from across the kitchen. Gathering myself, I went in the opposite direction and checked the section I was assigned before going out onto the floor.

The lunch rush had me constantly on the move, and I quickly got back into the swing of things. It was almost like I was never away and after a while, I was too engrossed in my work to be distracted by Rex or any of my problems. Even the other girls weren't being too nasty, besides Felicia, but at this point I was used to her cattiness and didn't take it to heart. Heavy's absence was probably the only reason none of them were doing too much, and that was mainly because he had some business to take care of. Before I knew it though, it was time to get off and I wasted no time tipping out and grabbing my stuff to leave with Rex right on my heels. Once we got to the door, he held it open for me and I was shocked to see Niko roaming around out front. As soon as he saw me, he began power walking in my direction only to be stopped in his tracks by Rex.

"What the—Adore! Tell this man to get his hands off me!" he shrieked, voice shaking fearfully. If I was him, I'd be afraid too, considering how big Rex was, and a small part of me wanted him to beat his ass.

"What do you want, De'Niko?" After the things he had his

lawyer saying in court, I didn't want to hear shit from him, but if hearing him out would get him from around me then I was willing to give him a few minutes of my time.

"Can you call your dog off?" his corny ass tried to joke, but it fell flat.

"Nope, but if you don't get to talkin' soon I'm gone sic him on yo' ass." My voice was sugary sweet and even Rex gave him a sinister smile that had him chuckling nervously.

"Okay, okay. I see you've spending a lot of time with uh, *Heavy*." He lowered his tone like he was scared somebody would hear, and I slowed my steps. "I don't know if you should be spending time with him considering the type of things he's into. You probably don't know that he's in business with my dad." He paused for dramatic effect but I kept my poker face on. There was a reason I wasn't involved in anything having to do with my brother and Heavy's business, and as far as I was concerned I didn't need to be. When he saw that his words weren't doing anything, he pressed on even though I was beyond done with the conversation.

"You don't wanna know why two people that seem to hate each other would go into illegal business together?" He raised his eyebrows like he was really expecting an answer, but I rolled my eyes, fed up with him already. Anything out of his mouth was questionable and I didn't even know why I'd allowed him any of my time. Honestly, I was more pressed about how the fuck he even knew where I was to be popping up.

"Let's go, Rex," I scoffed, and Rex gave Niko a hard shove that landed him on his ass before following behind me.

"It's because he's his son!"

My feet instantly halted and my throat tightened. I damn sure wasn't expecting to hear anything like that. How true it was, I had no idea, but after losing in court there was no telling how far he'd go to ruin my life. His father had already put a hit out on my life and while I knew he didn't have the balls for something like that, he'd still allowed this to go this far.

"Do you really think you can trust him, knowing his connection to my—*our* father?"

"Fuck you, Niko! Heavy has been there for me since day one and that's way more than I can say for your pathetic ass! Don't act like you honestly give a fuck about me. Keep the same energy you've had for the last eight years, and make sure Kaliyah's ready on Saturday. I'll be there at noon." Turning away, I ignored him calling out for me and finished the short trek to the car. I wasn't about to let him fuck up my life a second time, not when things were finally beginning to look up for me.

When we made it back to the condo, both Heavy and Kay Kay were already there sitting at the table. I couldn't help but smile seeing him helping her with her homework. It was the exact type of scene I'd envisioned back when I'd first found out I was pregnant. I used to imagine a life where it would be Niko doing things like that with our baby. Little did I know, my thoughts would come to fruition, just with another woman.

Shaking off my thoughts, I met Heavy in the center of the room. "Hey, how was yo' first day back?" he asked, giving me a quick peck and sliding my bag off my shoulder. Just like always, his touch had my stomach full of butterflies.

"It was...okay, I guess. The same as always." I shrugged, not wanting to bring up Niko's random visit at the moment, even though I knew Rex would more than likely tell him anyway. "I made some good tips though." I tried to perk up when I saw his brow dip slightly in concern.

"Okay, big money!" His face split into a grin, and I rolled my eyes at his corny ass. Even when I hustled my hardest and had a really good day at the restaurant, I didn't make anywhere close to what he just handed me for pocket change.

"Shut up!" I giggled, giving him a playful shove.

"Hey Adore!" Kay Kay gushed as I entered the kitchen area. She looked absolutely adorable with her hair in two long ponytails with bows.

"Hey baby, your dad doing a good job helping you with your homework?" I ran a hand gently over her head, trying to stifle my laugh when she rolled her eyes and sighed dramatically.

"Noooo, he keeps getting mad because he doesn't like our math!"

"Aye, slow me up, ayite! This new math weird as hell, they added a bunch of unnecessary steps," Heavy grumbled, joining us in the kitchen and pulling out a handful of takeout menus.

"Well, Mommy likes my math. Can we go see her? She can help." It seemed like everything stood still, and I looked at Heavy with my lips pressed together tightly. He still hadn't told her about Sha'ron being in the hospital since there hadn't been any change in her condition. I could understand him not wanting her to see her mom bruised up and attached to all types of machines, but it was obvious she missed her.

"Uhh, yo' mom's real busy with work right now, but as soon as she gets some free time she'll—"

"I know, I know. She's always busy." Disappointed, Kay Kay cast her eyes back down to her homework. Heavy and I awkwardly locked eyes and it was obvious that this was one of the only times he wasn't sure of what to do or say.

"You know what, I'm actually pretty good at math. Will it be okay if I help for now...until your mom is able to?" I shrugged, offering her a small smile.

"Okay." She didn't seem very happy about me being the

one to help, but at least she hadn't just told me no right off the bat.

"What about pizza for dinner?" The mention of pizza instantly had her mood shifting and she cheered happily, already turning into her regular talkative, upbeat self. Crisis averted for now, the tension left Heavy's shoulders as he went to call in the order.

CHAPTER SEVEN

HEAVY

I was still feeling like shit about keeping Sha'ron's condition away from Kay Kay, but as soon as I laid eyes on her in the hospital bed I knew I'd made the right decision. I stopped by the hospital after taking Kay Kay to school and immediately felt a pang of guilt. She was only in this situation because of me, and regardless of how much I couldn't stand her ass, she didn't deserve for anything like this to happen to her.

The steady beeping of the machines and the ventilator hissing were the only sounds that could be heard in the room, making it easy to get lost in my thoughts. I held on to Sha'ron's limp hand, silently trying to will her out of her coma. This was only my first time visiting since I'd found out that she wasn't dead like the bitch ass police tried to tell me. I was going to make sure to get at his ass too, along with anybody else Black had involved.

"Oh hell naw! Who the fuck let his ass in here! I want them fired right muthafuckin' now! How y'all gon' let the nigga that did this to her in her room?" I immediately recognized the voice of Sha'ron's aggravating ass mama and gently set her hand back down before standing. I wasn't at all surprised to see her sister, Sharita, there also, looking just as disgusted at the sight of me as their mother.

"Sandra, you know damn well I ain't do no shit like this! You been knowing me for years—"

"I don't know *shit*! All I do know is that my baby laid up in a hospital bed beat the fuck up and you was the nigga they found at her house that night!" she cut me off, and I had to stop myself from disrespecting her like she'd just done me. All of a sudden she didn't know my ass, but whenever she needed some shit I was the first number she dialed sometimes even before her own damn daughter.

"It ain't like you ain't never put yo' hands on her before! Yeah, she told me, and don't think I won't bring all this shit up as the reason why Kay Kay shouldn't be nowhere near yo' crazy, drug dealing ass!" I was across the room in record time and right in her face so she understood just how serious I was. Her already light skin immediately went pale and her eyes bucked.

"See, that's where you got shit fucked up. Not you or nobody else better even think about taking that little girl from me, or else you gone find out just how crazy my drug dealing ass *really* is."

"Is that supposed to be a threat?" Sandra tried to sound tough but her voice was too shaky to pull it off, and still facing her daughter, I looked her way with a sinister smirk.

"Take it how you want, I just know I better not hear shit else about Kaylani Stone being taken out of my care." Fear had them frozen in silence and my grin spread, satisfied.

"What's going on in here?" A nurse busted in the room, looking between the three of us expectantly, but I wasn't giving shit away.

"Nothin', I was just leavin'," I grumbled, pushing past Sharita and Sandra, making sure to shoulder check them both as I did. Pausing just as I reached the door, I turned around to say one last thing to the two. "Remember what I said though, ayite?" I wasn't waiting for a reply because the look on their faces was good enough.

I was still pissed off by the time I made it back home and I wasted no time putting in a call to my lawyer and a tail for Sha'ron's mama and sister. With John missing, I went ahead and accepted that he was dead and assigned a new nigga as my errand runner. I was sure Black had something to do with it, much like he did with everything else, I just didn't understand why. After I made sure I had Perry on the case drawing up temporary custody papers, I got ready to do my pickups. Quay was taking Isis to the doctor, so I was going to cover for him until I had to pick up Kay Kay from school.

"Hey, you're back already?" Adore came out of the bedroom in some of my joggers and a sports bra. She was out of breath and had a sheen of sweat on her chest and shoulders, letting me know she'd been doing her little workout. Ever since we'd moved into the condo, she'd been spending a half hour a day on the treadmill I had in the extra bedroom, and I had to admit she looked good as fuck drenched in sweat. It had me ready to take her down every time and now was no different.

"Hell yeah, and it look like I'm right on time too." I snatched her up as she made her way to the kitchen.

"Dominique, I'm sweaty as hell!" she shrieked, trying to wiggle out of my grip, but I held onto her slippery ass.

"So, it ain't shit that can't be washed off. Now give me kiss." Setting her down on her feet, I poked my lips out until she finally pressed hers against them. I slipped my tongue into her mouth, deepening the kiss until she moaned out loud and wrapped her legs around my waist. I had full intentions on just stopping through to change and run by the traps, but I may as well kill two birds with one stone. With our lips still locked, I carried her into the bathroom and set her on the sink as I leaned over and started the shower. It quickly became steamy, as we stripped out of our clothes and I attacked her lips again, lifting her in my arms. Carrying her into the shower, I immediately released her hair from the ponytail it was in. I loved the way it fell framing her face like a halo and absorbing the moisture.

We both released satisfied sighs as I slid inside her wetness, and my knees damn near buckled from the tight fit. Holding onto the tiled wall for support, I held onto her waist tightly as she dropped her head on my shoulder, already trying to give out.

"Nah, look at me while I'm givin' you this good dick," I commanded, and she instantly locked eyes with me, just like I'd told her. Biting into her lip sexily, she began fucking me back and her grip stiffened around my neck.

"Ooooh, fuck! Right there!" she let out a in high-pitched squeal.

"Just like that?"

"Yesssss, just like that!" Tossing her head back, she picked up the pace moving wildly, and her walls clenched around me, letting me know her orgasm was erupting. I let her go crazy, still keeping the same steady stroke. "Ooooh Dominique, I'm cumming!"

"Fuck, me too!" I panted, already feeling my balls beginning to tingle. As bad as I wanted to pull out, it was feeling way too good, and instead of doing so I buried myself deeper just as I exploded. Tucking my head in her chest, I propped her against the wall while we both held each other tightly and tried to recover. "You good?" I finally asked after a few seconds, and she chuckled.

"Shiiiiit, I'm great!" Her silly ass grinned lazily, and I just shook my head, giving her a quick peck as I lowered her to the floor.

"Yo' ass crazy, man." Shrugging, she eventually moved away from the wall and grabbed her loofah.

"A lil' dick crazy, but that's not all the way bad." She wasted no time squeezing on some bodywash and lathering her body. I loved how stress free she was these days. Always smiling and cracking corny ass jokes, and I just knew it would only keep getting better for her. Shaking off the soft ass shit I was thinking, I soaped up my own towel and began washing up myself. When I finished, I helped her wash her hair then rinse before we both climbed out.

Twenty minutes later I was dressed and ready to go, while Adore was sitting still wrapped in her towel as she blow dried her hair. That shit always took forever and I was glad she had Rex to drive her ass to work, because I wasn't trying to wait. My dick already had me late and I already knew niggas was gone have some shit to say about that.

"I'm out babe, I gotta make a couple plays. I'ma see you when you get off, ayite?" I bent to give her another kiss, with my thirsty ass.

"Okay, see you later." She cheesed, cutting her blow dryer back on so she could finish. It was becoming clear to me that I was addicted to shorty, because I was already regretting having to leave. That shit wasn't normal for me. When it came to money I didn't play around, but it was different with Adore. I was willing to leave a bag just so I could spend more time with her, and it wasn't even just all about the sex. I could literally just sit and watch a movie with her or play cards. Shit, everything I did with shorty was fun and it only made me want to be around her more.

I made it out of the apartment without doubling back and nodded at Rex who was already on guard in the hallway.

"Aye Heavy, let me holla at you." He fell into step beside me as I walked to the elevators. "I don't know if Adore told you or not, but the other night when she got off, that nigga De'Niko was outside her job talkin' crazy." The words had barely left his mouth and I immediately halted, ready to fuck him up. One for not telling me sooner, and two for even letting his ass get close enough to Adore that he could speak to her. Seeing the look on my face, he threw his hands up in surrender.

"What the fuck that nigga say?" I grit, uninterested in anything else.

"He uh...he was talkin' 'bout you and his pops workin' together." My brows dipped at that and I chortled bitterly. I could see his ass telling my fucking business and keeping himself out of it. Right away, I made up in my mind that I was going to make a special trip to see him just so I could kick his lame ass.

"Ayite man, I'ma handle it."

"Naw, that ain't it," he added, leaning closer and lowering his voice so his partner couldn't hear. After I motioned for him to go ahead, he finally said, "He told her that, that nigga yo' pops." Now I was really confused. I didn't understand what his ass thought he'd gain from that. As far as I knew, Sr. had never even told him, so for him to suddenly know and be going around telling Adore of all people was crazy as hell. I was going to make sure though that by the time I was done with him, he wouldn't ever mention that shit again.

CHAPTER EIGHT
QUAY

"And it looks like it's a...." Dr. Jones's ultrasound tech was taking all day to tell us our baby's gender and I was ready to knock everything off her little makeshift desk. I could see the grin on her face growing as she continued to move the machine around Isis's belly.

"Damn, do you know or not, shit? You got me feelin' like we need to call somebody else in here 'cause you gettin' on my nerves, bruh!"

"Oh my god, Quay, stop!" Isis laughed nervously, trying to lessen the blow from my words, but I was dead ass. I swear she was too nice at times, but I wasn't going to just let any ole body with a lab coat play us. She was definitely gonna hate me once the baby was here 'cause I was gonna act a whole fool.

"Nah, 'cause she over there playin' like muhfuckas ain't got shit to do! Give it here, I'll find the shit!" I didn't know why I was so pissed off, but it might've been because I'd heard that Manny hadn't taken heed to my warning and instead of getting his shit together was trying to sell some tainted ass shit using my name. I'd gotten word that at least five hypes had died behind whatever it was he was giving them, and since he was acting like he was still on my team, word had gotten around. The traffic around the trap had already started slowing down and I knew I was going to have to do something about his ass.

Isis was looking at me like she wanted to kill me while the ultrasound tech seemed shaken up. "Uhh, well there's no need for that, sometimes baby just doesn't want to cooperate—"

"You tryna blame my baby now?" I leaned forward with my face balled angrily as she began backtracking.

"N-no, no, I just mean if they're in a comfortable position they're less likely to move for the picture is all." Her tone grew high-pitched and her eyes bounced between me and the screen like she was afraid to take them off me. Since Isis was on the table thing between us she gripped my chin, forcing me to look at her.

"You okay?" she quizzed, eyebrows drawn in concern. I knew I had to be tripping if she was asking me if I was okay instead of cursing me the fuck out. This was honestly one of the rare moments I felt like she was being the old Ice, before I found out how sneaky she was. I still couldn't fully fuck with her like that after the shit she'd done though, but for the sake of my baby I wasn't completely giving her ass the cold shoulder.

"Oh, there he goes! It looks like you guys are gonna be having a boy!" ole girl damn near shouted before I had a chance to reply. My head whipped around to look at the screen so fast I almost got a neck cramp.

"You sure?" I didn't know what I was looking at as I watched her label the sonogram with *it's a boy*, but it did low key look like a dick between two legs.

"Yep, it's definitely a boy!" she repeated, pointing out everything on the screen. Isis's emotional ass was already

crying while I just sat there and took it in. My ass was about to
have a son out here! His ass hadn't even made it into the world
or taken his first breath and my chest was already swelling
with pride. I was even more excited now and ready to meet
him, knowing that I'd be doing everything in my power to be a
better man for him than my father ever was to me.

I was still riding on cloud nine when we left and stopped at
Church's Chicken for lunch. After giving me an order for damn
near the whole menu, I left Isis in the car while I ran inside.
Just like I expected, it was busy as fuck and it took forever
before I made it to the counter to place my order. The news
about my son had me much more patient than normal, so
instead of cursing them out for the long ass line, I ordered our
shit and went to stand off to the side to wait. Since it was going
to be a minute, I pulled my phone out and hit up Rock. He'd
finally gotten over his little hissy fit about Heavy and was
handling business as usual, which was exactly why I fucked
with him so tough. I let him know that I'd be through later so
we could try and find Manny. My head was still down, but I felt
a set of thirsty ass eyes on me and looked up to see Carmise. I
swear I almost said fuck the food, but I'd already paid and
since I was calling today a cheat day for Isis, I knew she'd be
ready to fight my ass if I didn't bring her this greasy ass
chicken.

As soon as she saw that I wasn't about to cut up on her, she
gained the courage to switch over to me and I blew out a frustrated breath. "Get the fuck from round me shorty, I ain't on
that shit today," I dropped my eyes back to my phone and said
as soon as she was within ear shot, and she immediately
sucked her teeth.

"Boy please! Ain't nobody worried 'bout you or yo' stupid
ass baby mama!"

"So what the fuck you over here for? Carry yo' funny lookin' ass back over there and get yo' food before my stupid ass baby mama come in and beat that wig off yo' head! I low key still owe you a bullet for even approachin' her anyway!" I growled, hoping she'd take heed to my warning, but, of course, she didn't.

"Tuh! How you gone shoot me 'cause you ain't got no self-control? I was really just tryna see if you wanted to come over still since it's been a while and I know Isis ain't keeping you satisfied, but I guess—" Her words got stuck in her throat when I snatched her ass up by the shirt and pulled her close to me. I made sure I got right in her face so she knew just how serious I was.

"I got an extreme amount of self-control or I would've started shooting as soon as I saw yo' simple ass! Hell no, I don't want to go to yo' crib! My baby mama makes sure to drain my balls multiple times a day and yo' pussy ain't nowhere near as good as hers! That pregnant pussy be bomb as fuck. Taste good too, how it smell though?" I asked, grinning as she squirmed to get away. Laughing, I shoved her dumb ass back a couple feet, enjoying the horror on her face from thinking I'd blown pussy breath right in her grill. She stumbled trying to get herself together and save face in front of the lone friend she had with her.

"See, I knew you were a goofy, but I ain't think you was stupid enough to come back for this work again."

"*Shit!*" I instantly pinched the bridge of my nose when Isis came inside the lobby looking beyond pissed. Thankfully, after that last ass whooping Carmise didn't want any smoke with her regardless of the shit she'd just been talking, but that wasn't going to stop my baby mama from showing her whole ass. Before she could advance on her, I was across the room wrapping her up in a bearhug that I found myself struggling with since her stomach was in the way. With my baby mama somewhat restrained Carmise took that as her opportunity to get away. "She gone Ice, damn! You ain't even s'posed to be on yo' feet let alone fightin' hoes in a fuckin' Church's!"

"Get yo' hands off me! I should be fightin' yo' ass for even givin' that stupid bitch the ammo! Just get my god damn chicken and come on!" She shook me off and I immediately released her so her ass wasn't struggling too much and stressing my baby out more than she was with the scene she was putting on.

"Get them fuckin' cameras off her man, what the fuck!" I shouted at the numerous people with their phones out recording. Of course, they wasn't paying my ass any mind, until I flashed the gun on my waist. Right then they called my number and the girl behind the counter hurriedly passed me my shit. It felt like I was doing a fucking walk of shame as I walked out behind a still grumbling Isis, and I just shook my head.

After I got Isis settled at home, meaning she snatched the whole bag of food and stormed up to her bedroom, I rode out in search of the right person to take my anger out on. I'd been serious when I said I'd kill his ass and he'd obviously taken me for a joke. I rode straight over to Blackstone first, even though it was unlikely that he'd be there after what he'd done. Still, I didn't want to leave no stone unturned.

Covering up the peephole, I banged on the door like the police, and a second later it was snatched open by his girl. The pissed off look on her face instantly turned to one of surprise at the sight of me. I pointed my gun right at her stomach and stepped inside, making her back up to give me room. "Where Manny?"

Sucking her teeth, she rolled her eyes up into her head. "His cheatin' ass gone! Probably with that hoe over on 79th livin' in that fuckin' roach motel!" She waved me off and tightened the short robe she was wearing, before narrowing her eyes on me. "Did you know his ass was fuckin' somebody else? 'Cause that's fucked up, Quay! Comin' over here callin' me sis and shit like we cool!"

"Maaaan," I scoffed, pushing her further up the hallway since she'd stopped walking to say that shit. I wasn't going to feed into her bullshit because I knew damn well that I hadn't given her any reason to think we were cool. Once we came into the living room, I looked around briefly while she continued talking shit. Eventually, I just went to check each of the bedrooms and she snapped out of her rant long enough to follow me.

"Hey, I said he ain't here!"

Ignoring her, I checked each of the closets and under the beds until I was satisfied that she was telling the truth. I knew how women were, and even if they'd been arguing about him cheating before I got there, she probably still would've hidden him from me if he asked.

"See, I told you. Since you're in here though, you might as well stay a while." She tilted her head and smirked up at me suggestively, causing my nose to turn up in disgust. Little did she know, I'd never stick my dick in anything after Manny and her even making the suggestion had me heated. My eyes landed on a lifting track in her head as I looked her over.

"You need to be more worried about finding some track glue and less worried about fuckin' me to get back at a dead nigga," I sneered, making the smile drop from her face. Leaving her standing there, I left and made it to my truck just as Heavy called. I knew he was probably trying to find out where I was since he was only covering for me while I went to the doctor with Isis and my impromptu mission to find Manny had me late. Even though I wasn't trying to hear his mouth, I still picked up just in case there was an emergency.

"Yo—"

"Nigga, why you ain't tell me about Manny?" he cut me off, getting straight to the point, and I couldn't do shit but shake my head. I'd been hoping to get a handle on things before I even needed to bring it to his attention, but obviously niggas had loose lips.

"My bad man, I thought I'd be able to fix it before it caused us any issues." Putting the phone on speaker, I pulled off into traffic more determined to find his ass than ever.

"Too late, word already gettin' around and a couple houses took a big loss," he said, and I grit my teeth angrily. "We need to regroup. I'll meet you at yo' crib at like....eight, after I put Kay Kay to bed."

"Ayite, bet." Ending the call, I pulled out the rest of my blunt from earlier and lit it immediately. Today had already been full of bullshit and I knew I'd probably need a bunch more weed and maybe even a bottle once it was finally over.

CHAPTER NINE
ISIS

"Oooh, that's cute, bestie!" I gushed over the outfit Adore held up into the camera to show me. She was going shopping for her visit with Kaliyah the next day, and despite being salty that I couldn't fully share in this experience with her I was putting up a good front. I was so happy for her finally being able to spend time with her baby and as nervous as she was, I could tell she was equally excited.

"Uhh, I don't know. It's giving Sunday brunch. I'm going for a more laid back look since they said I can take her to the museum." She placed it back on the rack and flipped the camera back around to her face.

"True, the last thing you wanna be doing is walking around a damn museum with heels or something on," I agreed. "I think a simple pair of jeans or sweats and a graphic tee will look cute with the right sneakers though. You're thinking too much into it. She's far from the stage where she'll be worried about what you have on, unless you're flooding or wearing some Mexican Jordans or some shit." I laughed and she joined in after a second, already knowing Kaliyah wouldn't be the only one with something to say if she was to wear those god-awful shoes.

"I can't stand you," she huffed, feigning an attitude. "That's why you're having a boy."

"Ha, jokes on you 'cause junior gone be right with his annoying ass twin! He ain't gone be driving me crazy." I was dead ass serious too. Since Quay was so happy about having a little mini me, then he could be the one toting him around once he was big enough to start raising hell like I knew he would after being genetically tied to his ass. Adore was cracking up laughing and I just knew the people inside Macy's was looking at her ass crazy just like I was.

"How you know he gone look like Quay? He could come out lookin' just like you," she pointed out, making me roll my eyes.

"I doubt it. The way yo' brother been gettin' on my last nerve, he's definitely going to look just like his ass." I wasn't necessarily bitter about having a boy, especially since Adore had Kaliyah, but I could feel it in my gut that he was going to be more his father than me. The way Quay immediately started acting let me know just how obsessed he was about to become about this little boy. I thought for sure he'd be dragging me to the mall after my appointment, but the scene at Church's had him dropping my ass right back at home and peeling out. *Ole ugly ass!*

"You crazy." She chuckled, shaking her head, looking just like her damn brother. "Oooh, what about this?" Instead of turning the camera around this time she simply held up the pair of army fatigue cargoes. I couldn't really see the whole thing but I could tell they had a lot of straps and embellishments hanging on them.

"That'd be cute with a black sweatshirt and some dunks." I was already nodding as the outfit came together in my mind.

"Yeah, I think so too," she said, pulling them away so she could take another look.

"Awww, I'm so happy for you boo!" Against my will, tears began clouding my vision and I hurried and tried to wipe them away.

"Not you cryin', old soft ass," Adore joked, even though her eyes were looking a little misty too.

"Oh well, you're just gone have to deal with it!" I teased, sticking my tongue out playfully. "Nah, but for real though, I'm just so glad you're getting everything you deserve, boo! A lot of people would've gave up with all the shit you had stacked against you, but you haven't let your circumstances keep you down and I'm so proud you're my best friend." I got choked up just thinking about how many odds were stacked against her.

"Awww, bestie!" She swiped away the tears that had managed to escape her eyes. "You got me in this store crying and shit, they gone think I'm crazy."

"Girl, fuck them! They can think what they want but they bet not say nothin' to you!" Quay would definitely have a fit, but if a bitch got out of line I'd gladly take the trip up there and beat their ass.

"I'm not bouta play with yo' bipolar ass. Let's just finish piecing this together so I can go grab her a couple things from Target too." She was already moving to the register and we ended up staying on the phone until she finished all her shopping. It wasn't quite like how we usually shopped together but it was close enough, and I was more than happy to lend my opinion.

When I finally hung up, I went down to the kitchen to grab something to eat. After such a long day I was far from in the mood to go to my store and do any type of work no matter how small. I was actually ready to take a nap but I wanted to eat a little bit more of my food since the events from earlier ruined my appetite a little. After thinking on it and talking to Adore, I realized I made myself angry for nothing. Carmise wasn't fucking with me on a good day. I'd let her take me out of my element and risk my baby's health for the second time, but there definitely wouldn't be a third. I wasn't even upset at Quay anymore and I pulled out my phone to call him. Of course, he didn't answer, but instead of just hanging up with an attitude, I decided to leave a message.

"Hey, it's me." Realizing how stupid that sounded, I rolled my eyes but kept going. "I'm not calling to yell at you or nothin', I just wanted to make sure you were okay and...apologize for trying to fight earlier. I shouldn't have let that bitch get me riled up and I'm going to do better about controlling myself so I can stay stress free. Okay, I love you...bye." I rushed to hang up, mentally chastising myself about everything I'd said and how I'd said it. It was like a word vomit though, because I hadn't expected to say half that shit. Shrugging it off, I continued to heat up my food. If he accepted then he accepted, but if not I wasn't tripping either. It was all about my baby's health at the end of the day.

Like a feign, I stood right in front of the microwave watching my food spin around on the glass tray. The smell quickly filled up the kitchen, making my stomach rumble hungrily, and I kind of wanted to take it out early, but the sound of the front door opening stole my attention. I raised a brow seeing Quay walking in with a lit blunt in his mouth. As happy as I was to see him in the house so early, I shuffled back to the kitchen without even speaking, like I hadn't even just told his ass I loved him on his voicemail. By the time I got there the microwave had stopped and I sprinkled a little bit of hot sauce on my chicken after pulling it out.

"You love me and you gone behave, huh?" Quay's tone was

full of amusement and it was evident on his face when I finally turned to face him.

"I did *not* say I'd behave, asshole!" My outburst only made his grin widen and his chinky eyes appeared closed from how low they were.

"Yeah, you did, you just said it in Isis language," he cracked, pushing himself off the wall he was leaning against.

"Yeah, ayite," I mumbled, grabbing my food and preparing to leave, but he stood in the way, filling my nostrils with the smell of his Dior cologne and strong ass weed. "Moooove! What yo' goofy ass doin'?" Frowning, I attempted to back away from his palm as he pressed it against my forehead.

"I'm just tryna see if you sick or some shit. Yo' ass ain't told a nigga you love him without my dick being involved in a minute, and you *never* apologize. So either my son got you trippin' or you sick, now let me see." He couldn't even keep himself from cheesing at the mention of our son. After the way he'd acted at the doctor's office that lady probably wasn't gone do another ultrasound for my ass, but I was still happy that he was so excited. I was sure he'd have acted the same way if she would've told us we were having a girl too, with his kid loving ass.

"I ain't sick, it's definitely yo' big headed ass baby. Now get off me before my chicken get cold!"

"Ayite, bet." He moved away, still smirking, and I found my face mirroring his until I got up the stairs. I didn't want to assume shit, but I couldn't help wondering if his change in attitude was because he'd just climbed out of another bitch's pussy. I had to tell myself he wasn't dumb enough to put his hands on me after fucking, but the thought had me abandoning my food and going back downstairs. He was still in the kitchen, now heating his own food up as he scrolled on his phone. At the sound of my footsteps, he looked up curiously since I probably looked crazy as hell. "What's up, Ice?"

"Did you just go fuck somebody else after you dropped me off?" Gasping, my eyes widened as a realization hit me. "Did you go fuck Carmise?" Head cocked, he narrowed his eyes and set his phone down on the counter before folding his arms.

"Where the fuck this shit come from? A second ago you was whining about yo' food getting cold and now you down here questioning me about Carmise? I swear to God yo' ass crazy, bro," he scoffed, grabbing his food out the microwave when it beeped.

"You didn't answer my question." Shifting from one foot to the other and crossing my arms, I tried to watch his body language for any signs of lying. He thought he was real slick with that deflecting shit, but I wasn't falling for it. Ignoring me, he went to grab a water bottle out of the fridge and went back to his food like I hadn't even said shit.

"You gone stand there and watch me eat?" he laughed, around a mouthful of food.

"You just gone stand there and not answer my question?" Shaking his head, he swallowed and took a long swig of water then wiped his hands on a paper towel.

"No man—"

"No, you not gone answer my question or no you didn't just fuck Carmise?" I inched closer as my breathing got shaky. I hadn't completely gotten over the shit with Carmise, but I wasn't as mad. However, if I found out he was still fucking that bitch, I was going to show my ass.

"I ain't fucked nobody." He frowned, pulling my rigid body against his. "Shit been fucked up and I figured it shouldn't be like that at work and at home. A nigga was just tryna have a chill night...that's all." Pouting, I finally melted into him, satisfied with his answer, and I could feel his laughter rumbling in his chest. "I swear you need a bag to carry yo' crazy around in, man," he joked.

"You carry it since you like it so much, punk." I punched him in the side with a giggle, just as the doorbell rang. Pulling away, I looked up at him because I damn sure wasn't expecting company and Ms. Deb had a key. "You expecting somebody?"

"Oh yeah, that's the stripper I got us for this threesome—"

"Boy, you got me fucked up!" I shouted, already turning to go and send whoever it was on their way, but he pulled me back. "Get off me before I beat yo' ass too!" Laughing, he let me go, throwing his hands up, and as soon as he did I went storming to the door with him right behind me. Worried that he was going to try and stop me, I hurried to twist the knob with my hands already balled into fists.

"Uhh, what's up ,Isis? Quay?" I sucked my teeth at the sight of Heavy and turned around to smack my laughing ass baby daddy before going to reheat my food. He played too fucking much!

CHAPTER TEN

ADORE

I played with one of the cut-up pieces of fabric on my pants and looked out the window at the building. It felt like I was about to throw up, and the longer I sat there the worse it got. Sure, Kaliyah seemed genuinely curious when she first met me, but what if the Blacks' hateful asses had filled her head with bad things about me? De'Niko had already gone out of his way to disapprove of any friends and family I'd suggested to supervise, so we ended up paying for a court appointed one. That made me even more nervous because I had to worry about them not liking me either.

"Aye, you got this." Heavy covered my hand with his and gave it a soft kiss. "You been waiting on this day for how long?" he mused, raising a brow.

"Eight, nine years." My voice came out in almost a whisper as I finally spotted Kaliyah standing next to a tall, older Black man. He wasn't exactly what I'd been expecting, but I could tell he was capable of chasing my ass down if I tried to run off or something.

"Exactly, so now's your chance. Quit being nervous and go

spend some time with yo' baby. I already know she's going to love you just like everybody else that comes in contact with you." Tearing my eyes away from Kaliyah's anxious face, I looked at him and simpered. He'd basically indirectly said he loved me. Full of emotion, I leaned over the center console and gave him a kiss.

"Thanks, baby." He had already been being super supportive all morning, then he'd sent me off with a pocket full of money and his own little gift for her, from him and Kay Kay. So I was saying it for more than just his current pep talk. I could admit that whether he actually said it himself, I was definitely in love with his sexy ass.

Just like I expected, he brushed off my gratitude with a "stop saying thanks for shit I'm supposed to do," but I still rolled my eyes as I climbed out and went to grab the gift bag from the backseat. After letting me know he'd be back in a couple hours, he pulled off, and I took a few deep breaths before approaching my baby with a smile. I didn't want to start crying and freak her out, but it was hard to stop my eyes from growing misty from finally being so close to her after all this time.

"Hi, are you Adore?" the man asked, putting his hand out for me to shake.

"Yep, and you are?"

"My name's Lee, and I'm sure you already know Ms. Kaliyah here. She's been very excited for you to get here," he whispered the last part, and I couldn't help beaming at the news as I crouched down to her height.

"Hey, Kaliyah. It's nice to see you again."

"Hi," she said shyly, dropping her eyes, and I immediately looked to Lee's old ass. Shrugging, he mouthed that she was nervous, and I lifted the bag I was holding.

"I, uhh, I brought this for you. Kay Kay even added something from her and her dad too." That emitted a smile as she grabbed the handle.

"Wait, I gotta different birthday too?" she wanted to know, and I couldn't help but laugh.

"Oh no, sweetheart, this is just something nice for you." I decided I'd let her carry it so she wouldn't think I was taking it back. The wind was tearing us up though and I knew it was time to go in. "We can sit inside and see what you got since it's so cold out here." She nodded happily and placed her hand in mine, making my heart skip. It felt so natural and when we finally made it inside I didn't want to let her go. We sat in the front with Lee not too far behind as she went through her bags ooohing and ahhing at each item she pulled out. I'd bought her a couple of outfits and some cute things from Claire's.

"Oooh, can I wear this today?" she gushed, holding up the furry unicorn backpack I'd bought her with a smile.

"Yeah, you can even put a couple of your things inside. That way you won't have to carry this big bag around." I helped her transfer her lip-glosses and other little trinkets into the backpack and she immediately put it on. "Oooh, you look good Kali!"

"Kali?"

"Oh, I'm sorry, it's just a nickname, baby. If you don't want me to call you that then—"

"Oh no, I like it!" She smiled widely as Lee looked on in approval.

"Well, Kali it is." Seeing her so excited had me wondering what I'd been nervous for in the beginning. Just like De'Niko had said, she was great, and I couldn't wait to show her the rest of the museum.

At first she was pretty quiet, but after a half hour of pictures at the different exhibits she had loosened up. She was telling me all types of stuff about herself and a few other people. I quickly learned that gossiping was not something only Kay Kay liked to do.

"Yeah, I don't like my teacher Ms. Green either. She's really strict just like Farrah. She wouldn't let me have my fidget spinner in class 'cause she said it's distracting," she huffed as we made our way around the floor light exhibit, and the little pout on her face almost made me laugh, but I held it in and wrinkled my nose instead.

"What's a fidget spinner?" She stopped mid-step and looked up at me like I had two heads. I had went through a shit ton of toys with Kay Kay and on my own, so if I had heard it I definitely didn't remember, but the look on her face had me feeling real dim witted.

"You don't know what a fidget spinner is?" she asked for clarification, and I shook my head no. "Oh lord! I'm gonna have to bring mine next time to show you. It's gonna be a next time, right?" My heart melted right in my chest seeing her looking up at me hopefully, and my words got caught in my throat.

"Yeah, of course, it's gonna be a next time! You're really cool and I like hanging out with you, Kali," I said, nudging her.

"I like you too! I'm gonna tell all my friends how cool you are and how you dress really cute." I felt flattered considering how judgmental I knew kids could be, and I couldn't wait to tell Isis and Heavy. We spent the rest of our time taking more silly pictures and getting to know each other. Before I knew it Lee was looking at his watch and waving us over. Even though I knew we only had a few hours, I was still very disappointed to know our time together had come to an end and it would be a week before I saw her again. She seemed just as sad as me about it as we walked over to Mr. Lee hand in hand.

"Is it really time to go?" she pouted, and he nodded, giving her a sympathetic smile.

"It is, but next week you and Adore will be seeing each

other again and going somewhere else fun. Would you like that?"

"Yes! I can't wait! Thanks, Adore!" She threw her arms around me, and I hugged her back tightly, glad that she enjoyed my company and was excited to see me again. Too afraid to ask if I could walk them to his car, I just watched until they disappeared down the street before finally making my way to Heavy's truck where he was waiting on me with a bouquet of roses. As soon as I was close enough, he held them out to me.

"I take it from that big ass smile that today went well?" he questioned, giving me a quick kiss and pulling me into an embrace.

"Yep, and she's excited about next week already too!" I squealed, bouncing giddily. I truly felt accomplished just from the little bit we'd learned about each other. Soon she'd be telling me secrets and spending the night and calling me mama, and I couldn't wait. Leaning back, Heavy smirked down at me.

"Is that so? See, I told you she was gone love you."

"I knooooow, and it was so easy to get her talking. She told me all about her teachers and her extracurriculars. Oh, and she loved the stuff I bought her. She put the backpack on right away." I was talking fast and Heavy was hanging on to my every word, completely interested in everything I was saying.

"That's what's up, we gone have to figure out something even better to win her over next week. Maybe an indoor water park or something? You know kids love to play in water!" We shared a laugh because they definitely loved anything that had to do with water.

"Yeah, she'd love that for sure. I'll see if I can send word for them to pack her a swimsuit, as long as Lee is okay going there." I hadn't really considered that, but he probably wouldn't like a loud ass pool. Then again, this was what he got paid for so he might not mind.

Frowning, he pulled away enough to ask, "You talkin' 'bout that old nigga?" I didn't want to but I couldn't help the laughter that was threatening to bubble up in my throat.

"He's not that old."

"Shiiiit, that nigga geriatric, but I'm sure they gone let you. In the meantime, let's go celebrate, Kay Kay staying with my OG. I'll take you to the Sugar Factory so you can get one of those smokey ass drinks you like." Squealing like a little kid, I kissed him deeply.

"Ooooh, you tryna get some pussy tonight, huh?" I teased, even though I was definitely throwing this pussy on him when we got home.

His cocky ass just shrugged with a grin and opened the door for me. "I was gone get that anyway." An instant shiver went down my spine in anticipation.

CHAPTER ELEVEN
HEAVY

I still hadn't forgotten about the shit Rex had told me by the next week, and even though I had more pressing issues to take care of, I was going to make time to beat De'Niko's ass. I had my OG picking up Kay Kay while I sat camped outside of that nigga's office, ready to catch him as soon as he came out. Checking the time again, I saw that once again he was staying later than everybody else, and I couldn't help wondering if he somehow knew I was out there. After calling himself pulling up on Adore and telling my damn business he should've been expecting a visit from me anyway, but his daddy had him feeling invincible, like he couldn't be touched. I was about to prove that theory wrong though, whether he came out or if I had to go up to his office to get him. Low key, I was still wondering why Adore hadn't said anything to me about it. Even though I wasn't ready to admit that the mayor was my father for obvious reasons, I didn't want her thinking I was keeping shit like that from her. She had too many people in her life that had lied to her and set her up for failure, and I wasn't trying to be another disappointment. Shit had been going so well for her that I refused to ruin it. If she didn't bring it up to me then I wasn't going to say shit to her. Besides, soon enough his ass would be dead anyway so it wouldn't even matter.

Seeing movement across the way, I stepped out of my car making sure to close my door lightly. De'Niko was walking through the parking lot on his phone, totally oblivious to his surroundings. It was clear he was talking to his wife just from the way his bitch ass was whining.

"I'm not messing with anyone Farrah, I really needed to work late! You know what, I'm not doing this with you. I'll see you when I get home!" He hung up just as he got to his BMW, and I chuckled loud enough for him to hear. By now I was so close to him that when he turned around, we were damn near chest to chest, if he was a foot taller.

"D-D-Dominique," he stammered, stumbling back a few steps. His already pale skin looked ghostly white, and I almost felt bad for his scary ass.

"Yeah, Dominique. I guess since you know that we're brothers you feel comfortable callin' me by my name now, huh?"

"N-no." His ass was stuttering so bad, I almost felt bad about the ass whooping I was going to lay on him. Almost.

"It's cool, big bro, I'm only here 'cause you decided to go run yo' mouth about some shit that wasn't yo' business to tell. Shhhh," I quieted him as soon as I saw his mouth beginning to move to excuse what he'd done. "You been man enough to do all this other shit then you're definitely man enough to catch these hands." His eyes immediately dropped to my hands as I cracked my knuckles in preparation.

"Look, I, uhh, I didn't mean to cause any trouble. I just thought Adore deserved to know just like I did for all these years. I—oww! You hit me!" He held his cheek, trying to shake off the pain.

"I did tell you I was bouta rock yo' shit! You're the one tryna have a counseling session. Put yo' fuckin' fists up, *big bro*!" I taunted, taking a step toward him, but instead of doing what I told him he threw his hands up to protect his face, leaving his stomach wide open.

"Ohhh!" He doubled over, now holding his midsection, and I used the opportunity to hit his face with a two-piece that dropped him flat on his back. "Okay, okay!" he shouted and balled into the fetal position as I got closer. I wasn't planning on hitting him though. Grabbing two handfuls of his suit jacket, I bent down into his now bloody face and briefly admired my handy work. It had been a hot little minute since I'd actually used my fists, and it felt good that the first time in a while was on my deadbeat's other son.

"I'm lettin' you walk away *this* time, but if you keep fuckin' with Adore you won't have to worry about who knows about yo' pops' hoein' ass! Understand?"

"Y-yeah."

"*Promise*?" I teased, lifting a brow and growing even more entertained by the confusion on his face, until I shook him a little. "Nigga, say you promise, the fuck!"

"Okay, I promise! I promise!" Smiling, I let his ass go, and he fell against the concrete hard enough to make him groan. Pleased with the amount of damage I'd caused, I stood to my full height.

"Good, I don't need to tell you that this stays between us, right?" He looked up at me pitifully, with his lips in a grim line. I hoped he understood just how serious I was. As much as I hated his bitch ass, I didn't want to see him dead right along with his daddy. Straightening my clothes, I stepped right over his body and headed back to my car.

It had been a minute since I'd stopped through my OG's spot, so I decided to slide on her and grab me a plate. As soon as I came in, Felicia and the other thirsty ass staff immediately perked up and broke their necks to speak to me. Just like always, I hit them with a stiff head nod and swaggered back to my mama's office. She was sitting at her desk with her glasses perched up on her nose as she read over some paperwork. Tapping the door, I came in and dropped into the seat across from her.

"Ohhh, to what do I owe this pleasure?" she teased, leaning back in her seat with a grin.

"Damn, I can't just wanna come see my mama?" The look she gave me had my ass laughing, because she just knew I was full of shit.

"Nope, yo' ass probably just came to get these lil' girls in a tizzy before you go home to Adore." I palmed my chest and feigned shock, making her roll her eyes.

"Mannn, you know I don't want none of these hoe—I mean, girls. I'm good where I'm at."

"You better be." Ever since the day Adore stepped foot in Pam's, my mama had taken a liking to her and I noticed that shit right away. It wasn't like she was particularly mean, but the difference in the attention she gave shorty was obvious. She'd never even fucked with Sha'ron that way past the point of her pregnancy. Knowing what I know now, I completely understood. My OG could see the real in people even when I couldn't. That's why I was so happy about the relationship Adore had with her and Kay Kay. If my two leading ladies fucked with you then that had to mean something, because they weren't the easiest to impress.

"Mmmhmm. Kay Kay told me about her mama still being busy at work." She quickly shifted the conversation, making my smile drop instantly. I wasn't ready to talk about that shit, but judging from her body language that's exactly what we were about to do.

"Have you seen her? Shit, I'm still traumatized so I know my baby gone be. I ain't tryna fuck her up like that. Then Sandra up there hollering about how I shouldn't be able to see her and they're gonna try to take custody." Besides to get Perry on it, I hadn't much thought about the threat since I'd already warned them about what I'd do if they went through with it, but bringing it up to my mama had it right back on my mind.

"Tuh! A judge wouldn't dare give that baby to that heffa or her illiterate ass daughter! The only one with a little bit of sense is Sha'ron, and I don't even think she'd want her with their asses!"

"It won't even get that far if I got anything to do with it." The meaning was evident, and she nodded solemnly, tucking her lips into her mouth.

"Well, at least let Kay Kay go see her. She's not showing any activity and the last thing you want to do is have that girl thinking that her mama abandoned her when she really died. Did you even find out what happened to her yet? The police haven't got any more leads." I avoided her eyes for a minute and stroked the short hair on my chin. I still hadn't told her shit about me fucking with De'Niko and with good reason, but I didn't know how long I'd be able to keep that shit from her. She'd fuck around and kill his ass herself if she knew what all he had going on.

"Nah, I haven't heard shit yet, but if you think it's best then I'll take Kay Kay up there. I just need to figure out how to tell her first, ayite." She looked at me hard for a minute before sighing.

"Alright Dominique, just don't take too long. I can't imagine how my grandbaby gone feel if she loses her mama and don't know why." She clearly wasn't letting up while I was still stuck on how the fuck I was going to explain why her mama was in the hospital. Even Adore was feeling some type of way about me not saying shit to her; I could tell from the way she looked at me the day Kay Kay brought up Sha'ron. Neither of them understood the type of guilt I felt for what happened though. I think my biggest issue was knowing that her being in the hospital was a direct result of me, and the last thing I wanted was for my baby to blame me for what happened.

"Look, I can already see you overthinking. Kay Kay is a strong little girl, but I know she can handle this. That's how y'all raised her." I agreed. Sha'ron and I had done an amazing job with our daughter, and she was more emotionally stable than a lot of adults. I just wanted to make the right decisions when it came to her.

"Ayite, you're right Ma, now can I get a couple plates to go? I ain't had none of yo' cookin' in a minute." I patted my stomach for emphasis as I changed the topic to something a little lighter, and she instantly cheesed.

"You're lucky, I got a little bit of stuff put to the side already." She was already climbing out of her chair, and I followed suit.

"Yeah ayite, I was gone get some even if I had to take it out the big pot," I cracked, and she stopped walking, making me run right into her. "Nah, I'm just playing Ma. Come on."

"You better be." Wrapping my arm around her neck, I barely felt the tiny elbow she sent into my side as we headed out to the kitchen. After getting us a few plates of the day's special and a big bowl of chili for the next day, I was on my way home, still thinking of how and when I was going to tell my baby about her mama.

CHAPTER TWELVE
DE'NIKO JR

A week later I was still in pain after Dominique's animalistic attack. I was hurting all over like I'd been hit by a damn car, and Farrah's nasty attitude was only making it worse. She was moving around the kitchen slamming cabinets and pots around like I wasn't sitting there with a swollen head.

"Could you please stop banging around so much?" Wincing, I gripped the edge of the table and clenched my teeth. She grumbled something under her breath and slammed my plate down in front of me, completely disregarding my request. I wasn't in the mood to argue with her, which was clearly what she wanted. It was the weekend so Kaliyah was due to have her visit with Adore and that always put her in a bad mood. The more Kaliyah talked about her mother the more unhinged Farrah became, feeling as if she was being replaced.

As if I'd spoken her up, my baby came bouncing into the kitchen with the furry backpack that Adore had bought her slung over her shoulder. Despite the pain I was in, I smiled as she came over and placed a kiss on my cheek. "Good morning, Daddy!"

"Good morning, honey."

Oblivious to Farrah's mood, she sat across from me with her iPad and began watching her little ASMR videos. She looked just like Adore with her hair pulled up into a ballerina bun with a curly side bang hanging into her face. Today they'd planned to dress, alike according to Kaliyah, with matching hairstyles, t-shirts, and joggers. The week before when she'd presented the idea, Farrah's head damn near exploded. In her mind she was Kaliyah's mother, and it seemed like in a matter of weeks Adore had come and changed that. Honestly, at this point, I didn't see the harm in their relationship. If my family hadn't gone so hard to keep her away things would've never gone so far. Now the whole world knew that she wasn't me and Farrah's child and also knew I'd messed around with Adore while she was in high school. Although my business had yet to be effected, my dad's mayoral career was definitely over. I wasn't sure what he could do to win the voters back over but if I had to guess, it was nothing.

"Kaliyah, cut that annoying mess down now! You know I don't like smacking at the table!" Farrah damn near tossed her plate on the table and moved back over to the stove in a huff. She was really on one and even though I didn't want to argue in front of Kaliyah, I had to say something.

"Farrah, can I speak with you in the other room please?" It was more of a command than a request and she quickly caught on. I was already moving toward the dining room and after a few seconds she came traipsing behind me.

"What do you want? I'm trying to cook," she hissed, folding her arms as soon as I closed the door behind us.

"I wanna know what your problem is. You're around here

slamming shit around the kitchen and yelling at my daughter—"

"*Your* daughter, huh?" Her eyes bucked and I realized my mistake, but instead of admitting it, I pulled one of my dad's moves.

"If you're her mother then act like it! You can't expect her to want anything to do with you when you're being such a snarky bitch! Hell, I barely want to have anything to do with you these days." It was true. I was spending as much time as I could at the office and it wasn't even just to fuck Natasha. I hated that it was even the weekend so I didn't have anywhere to go, but if I was going to be in the house with her then I wasn't going to be dealing with her ridiculous attitude.

"Oh go to hell, De'Niko!" She went to walk off but I snatched her back by the ugly ass sweater she was wearing.

"This ridiculous pity party ends *today*! You will go out there and have breakfast with your family and you will be respectful to me and our daughter! Do you understand?" Her face was tight as she looked at me with glistening eyes, and I thought she was going to start with her crying again, but she busted into laughter instead.

"I really can't take you serious with those two black eyes!" she cackled, doubling over and holding her stomach like she'd just said the funniest thing in the world. Rage boiled inside me at her disrespect and I clenched my fist, prepared to give her a matching black eye. "Maybe if you would've had this much aggression when you were attacked, you wouldn't be walking around looking like a raccoon!"

I hadn't told her that Heavy was my brother, let alone that he was the one who'd attacked me. Only that I was robbed at gunpoint by two guys, which was how I accounted for the damage. Of course, she probably knew I was lying since I didn't go to the police, but she never voiced it out loud and that was fine with me. I didn't want to be further questioned about it because my story would fall apart and I'd have to tell her everything. She was still a ball of giggles when I left her there so I could drop Kaliyah off at the Child Protective Services office. Her eyes were on me the second I returned to the kitchen area and I immediately felt bad because I was sure she'd heard everything that was going on.

"Come on honey, I don't want you to be late meeting your —Adore," I quickly corrected. If she heard my mistake, she didn't show it and I was grateful for that. She might have known that Adore was her birth mother but she still considered Farrah her mother too. Even though she was a bitch, I didn't want Kaliyah to completely write her off. Hearing Adore's name had her smiling hard as she jumped up from her half-eaten breakfast and went to put her iPad away. Farrah always made a big deal about her taking her expensive things out with her like she wasn't being supervised by a whole professional whenever she left.

"I'm ready, Daddy!" She was back before I knew it with her jacket ready and I helped her slip it on, making sure to zip it all the way up to her neck.

"Okay, now you're ready."

I walked her out to our heated garage and opened the door for her before sliding into the driver's seat, happy that Farrah's ass had found somewhere to collect herself. More than likely, it was our bedroom, as usual. Pulling off, I immediately began feeling better and I knew it was because I was out of the house with her. Our marriage was mostly for show these days, but I was actually starting to get weary with putting on appearances anyway.

"Was Mom mad?" Kaliyah asked as soon as we left our gated community. I locked eyes with her in the rearview and forced a reassuring smile.

"Oh no, Mom's just not feeling too good, that's all. By the time you come back, I'm sure she'll be in a much better mood," I lied. For sure, Farrah's attitude would be significantly worse upon her return. The more time Kaliyah spent with Adore the more she talked about her, and that always set Farrah off. She wouldn't overtly take it out on our daughter, but her dry responses and the cold shoulder were obviously enough for Kaliyah to take notice. The look she gave me let me know that it wasn't a good lie, but she was already on to the next question.

"Is it because I'm going to see Adore?" Shifting uncomfortably in my seat, I put my attention on the road as I tried to conjure up sincerity.

"*What?* Of course not, she's happy you reconnected with Adore. Maybe she's just sad because she can't come too. I'm always a little sad that I can't go have fun with you guys too."

I could feel her eyes on me trying to figure out if I was serious or not, but I didn't dare meet her gaze. In addition to being extremely smart, Kaliyah was also very intuitive. Then again, her insight could be because she heard a lot of things and asked a lot of questions.

"Well, maybe next time you can come. Adore is really fun. Today is mommy-daughter match day though, so it's just supposed to be us."

"That's great, but your visits with Adore are actually just for the two of you, so Mom and I can't go. We'll start doing something on another day, as a family though. Would you like that?" Instead of the excited cheer I was expecting she simply shrugged, and I couldn't deny that my feelings were a little hurt. I didn't let it show, but when we finally made it to the hand-off location, I was relieved to get her little ass out of the car. I damn near burned rubber out of the parking lot and as soon as I was a safe distance away, I called Natasha. It had been a while since I'd needed her services, but after the week I'd had it was mandatory.

After getting my balls drained by Natasha, I strolled in the house almost two hours later. I was actually in a rush now, because it was almost time to get Kaliyah, but I needed to take a quick shower. Of course, Farrah was nowhere in sight, which was good for me, but her disappearing acts hadn't gone unnoticed.

I'd barely made it all the way inside though, when my doorbell rang. Cursing under my breath, I ran to answer it, hoping that whoever it was didn't take up too much of my time since I was already cutting it close. The last person I expected to see on the other side was my father, and I immediately wished that I'd ignored it.

Turning his nose up, he looked me over in disgust. "What the hell happened to your face?" He gripped my chin and moved my head side to side so he could further inspect the damage.

"Good afternoon to you too, *Dad*." I snatched away and backed up to allow him entry.

"Don't get cute, De'Niko. What happened to you? Is this the reason I haven't spoken to you in weeks?" Shoving his hands in his pockets, he turned to face me. "Are you on drugs?"

The ridiculous accusation had me chuckling as I shook my head bitterly. Only my father would think that my distance from him had anything to do with drugs as opposed to the shit I'd witnessed between him and my mother, among other things.

"You're fucking crazy, of course I'm not on drugs. Maybe you should see if your *other* son is." Scoffing, I moved past him and into the living room so I could pour myself a shot. These days our conversations always required some alcohol.

"Oh please, son, how dare you judge me when you're in the

same boat. Just because the circumstances aren't the same doesn't mean that you didn't cheat also. It's what every man in power does and will continue to do as long as there's willing pussy around. You're actually worse than me because you allowed your fiancée to take on the job of raising your indiscretion." By the time his little spiel was done, I'd swallowed my first shot and was already pouring another, but I paused and shot an evil look his way.

"*You* made me do that! Don't act like it wasn't some big scheme all along for you to appear to have the perfect American family! I didn't want to be a father!" I couldn't believe he was really throwing this shit in my face after forcing me to take in a child I never wanted and orchestrating this whole thing.

"Well, what did you propose we do? Let her poverty-stricken, teenaged mother take care of her and eventually grow bitter once she saw you with Farrah and spill the beans anyway? Or how about she grew up without you and decide once she's an adult to tell all of her family secrets online? I did what needed to be done! The only thing I actually messed up on was not killing that bitch when I had the chance! None of you know how far I've gone for this family!" his voice thundered, and he pointed a stiff finger my way. Over his dramatics, I waved him off and continued to pour my drink.

"If that's what helps you sleep at night, Dad." After draining my glass I poured another. He was pissed and just staring at me through narrowed slits, probably more worried about how much alcohol I'd consumed than what I was saying.

"I'm not going to argue with you, Jr. Tell me what happened to you!" I was sure he didn't want to know that the reason I'd gotten my ass whooped was because I'd gone to Adore and ran my mouth about him being Heavy's dad and also their business dealings. It was clear he wasn't going to let it go though.

"I was mugged."

"*Mugged?*" he repeated the word in disbelief, frowning as if it put a bad taste in his mouth.

"Yes, mugged, okay, and no, I don't wanna talk about it."

As if I hadn't even just said anything, he pressed me for more answers. "When? Where did this happen? Did you report it? Of course you didn't or else I would've known." Suddenly realization covered his face. "Was it that bitch's thug brother?" I swear you'd think Adore had killed his mother the way he hated her. I wasn't the biggest Adore supporter either but the vitriol my family had was wild to me.

"No, of course not. It happened outside of the office, you know it's been getting worse down there." He looked at me like he was trying to determine if I was telling the truth, and I rolled my eyes. "Anyway, what do you want, Dad? I need to pick up Kaliyah soon." I lied again because I was already late now.

"I stopped to let you know that we need to get rid of anything linking us to Dominique. Emails, call logs, paper-work, everything, and we need to do it fast. Even on his end. I got a feeling that he's going to try to pull something, and before he does I'm going to have his ass locked under the jail." Hearing my brother's name instantly had me tensing up and ready to pour another drink. I wasn't trying to have anything to do with whatever my father had going on, but just to buy myself some time I agreed. Pleased, my dad wasted no time leaving the way he'd come while my heart pounded out of my chest.

CHAPTER THIRTEEN
QUAY

I snuck out the door, being careful not to make too much noise, and climbed in the car with Rock. The shotgun I had resting inside my pant leg was uncomfortable as fuck and wasn't giving a lot of space to move, but it was my weapon of choice and I wasn't changing it no matter how uncomfortable I was.

"What up, bro?" he asked, clearly in a much better mood than the last time we'd been together.

"What's good?" We shook up and he pulled out of my driveway. I'd finally gotten a location on Manny and I was ready to go. He probably thought for sure by now that I wasn't coming for him, but he had to be a damn fool to believe that.

"You sure you got yo' info straight?" Rock asked as he drove, glancing between me and the road. Here he went asking a bunch of questions again, making my ass itch. I wasn't about to go down that road with him when I knew it'd start a fight.

"Yeah, it's verified," was all I told him. Honestly, I'd been the one who'd done the recon on this because it was my fault. I'd let Manny slide with a warning only for him to still turn around and fuck me, so now it was really fuck him. When Heavy had come over he'd told me that Hector somehow found out about the bad batch Manny had dispersed under my name, which made it an even bigger problem. That nigga obviously had friends in high and low places, unless he'd been following us, and I didn't like the thought of either being true.

"Ain't no fuckin' way," Rock grumbled, pulling me out of my thoughts, and I realized we'd arrived. He looked up at the building with his face twisted up and I knew exactly what he was thinking. The shit was a straight bomb and looked abandoned, but that was where Manny had been staying. I'd followed him there three times just to be sure that his ass actually lived there and wasn't just serving more of that bullshit out of it. It was crazy that a simple misunderstanding had caused us to fall out like this, but one thing I wasn't going to do was die or get hemmed up behind his shit.

"I said the same shit, but that nigga definitely in there." Adjusting the huge gun, I climbed out with my hand wrapped around the handle, not even waiting for him as I crossed the street, pulling my ski mask down with my free hand. For as fucked up as the building was it had a lot of residents that could identify our black asses. I never fell for that code people spoke of and I wasn't trying to take a chance on someone seeing my face. When I turned around to see if Rock was following, I saw that he was with his mask on too.

We entered the front door and I immediately directed him to follow me as I started down the stairs. The person that owned the building had decided to even use the basement for apartments and that's where Manny's was. Thankfully, there were only two apartments down there and the neighbor worked nights, so there was a better chance that we wouldn't be seen. Once we reached the landing, I crept up to his apartment door and listened for any sounds of movement inside.

When I didn't hear anything, I backed away and pulled my gun out, nodding for Rock to kick the door down. This nigga damn near knocked the shit off the hinges and I wasted no time running inside. It was a studio so as soon as we stepped in we were in the kitchen, living room, and bedroom at the same time. Even in the damn near pitch-black room I could see Manny jump off the bed and dive to the floor. I wasn't going to play hide and seek with his ass though. Searching for the light switch, I flipped it on, shedding a dim hue over the room and instantly making him visible. He was sliding across the floor trying to get behind the couch, and I fired, hitting him in the back. The shot instantly had his body convulsing, and I quickly made my way across the room to stand over him. Without even thinking about it, I hit him in the head, making it explode completely.

"Nigga, let's go!" Rock called out, pulling me toward the door. With the gun at my side we both ran, making it to the building's entrance as screams and footsteps began sounding from the apartments above us. When we got in the car Rock pulled off doing the dash until we were a safe distance away, eventually jumping on the freeway and blending into the other cars there. We made it to the cleanup spot and got rid of our clothes, the guns, and the car. It took much longer than I thought, and by the time he dropped me back off at the crib the sun was already beginning to come up. I was thankful that my son had Isis sleeping so damn hard, because she was still knocked the hell out. She was still sleeping in the guestroom and that made it even easier for me to move around. After a quick but thorough shower I immediately fell asleep as soon as my head hit the pillow.

I woke up to the sun shining in my damn face and my dick disappearing down Isis's throat, making my toes curl. Locking eyes with me, she continued to bob her head up and down as she stroked the base of my dick with one hand and cupped my balls with the other. Her ass was tooted up with her gown just barely covering it, and my dick hardened just thinking about how wet I knew she was. My baby mama was a real freak and sucking dick always had her pussy sopping wet and creaming for me.

"God damn, Ice! Come put that pussy on my face, I'm tryna taste it." Still sucking, she wagged her finger at me like she wasn't going to do what I'd said. After teasing me for a few seconds though, she finally twisted around so that her ass was in my face, and just like I expected she was pantyless. Licking my lips at the sight of her slick juices coating her fat pussy lips, I grabbed ahold of both her thick ass thighs and slithered my tongue through her slit. Her body stiffened instantly as I went to work sloppily tongue kissing her clit.

"Oooh baby, wait!" she begged, trying to reach back toward me but I slapped her hand away.

"Why my dick not in yo' mouth, Ice?" I taunted, knowing that a sixty-nine was gone have her ass unable to finish. It never failed that when my tongue got to work she could never handle it.

"Oh fuck! I'm tryyyying!" She was already panting as she hovered over my head, only managing to suck the tip before an orgasm took over and she began grinding against my face.

"Mmmhmm! Cum all on daddy face!" I coached, ready to bust just from how excited she was getting. Her moans grew louder as she quickened her pace and her juices coated my face from my nose down to my chin.

"Quuuay, I'm cummin', ahhhh!" Squeezing her ass cheeks, I held her in place, lapping up every bit of her juices even after her body had stilled. She laid on my chest trying to gather herself, but I wasn't done yet.

"Get yo' ass up off my son and ride this dick, Isis! *You* woke *me* up, ain't no rest shorty!" Despite the awkward position, I was able to slap her ass hard, making her moan sexily as she lifted herself up. Freak ass slid her wet pussy down my chest and stomach before inching down my shaft with her back still turned. "Fuuuuuck!" I couldn't help but moan feeling the inside of her walls swallowing me up. Leaning forward, she rested her hands on my thighs and began snaking her body slowly. From my angle all I could see was her ass jiggling, and I spread her cheeks apart, giving me access to her tight asshole.

"Ahhh fuck, Quay, you're not playin' fair!" she whined, putting more of an arch in her as I eased my thumb in her ass. I could already feel her walls choking the shit out my dick, and my balls tingled.

"God damn baby, you ridin' the fuck out me." Grunting, I squeezed my eyes closed, trying hard not to succumb to the sound of me slipping in and out of her coupled with her soft moans. Before I knew it another orgasm was rocking her body, but she continued to whine and that coupled with her walls contracting had me shooting off inside of her. My nut was so long and hard that I knew if she wasn't already pregnant that would've been the one to do it. Completely soft, my dick slipped out of her and she fell on the bed beside me still breathing hard.

"You got pussy all over yo' face," she cracked after staring at me for a few minutes, and I busted out laughing right along with her. I for sure thought her ass was about to say something cute like all women tried to do after sex, but I should've known better. Isis was a different breed.

"It's yo' pussy tho'. If yo' ass could handle head then you'd have nut all over yo' shit too," I shot back with a raised brow.

"You got me, but in my defense you be working the shit out yo' tongue." The way she sighed and closed her eyes I knew she was having flashbacks, and I grinned cockily.

"Long as you know." I gave her a pointed look and she sucked her teeth playfully, mumbling a whatever and snuggling closer. It was moments like this and the other day in the kitchen that had me forgetting about all the bad shit between us. There were times we'd be good as fuck and then I'd remember that she fucked with my enemy and killed one of my babies. It would put me in a fucked-up mood and I'd pull away, but I fought to keep those thoughts in the back of my mind as she laid on my chest. Resting my palm on her belly, I closed my eyes and noted how much more comfortable this was than sleeping alone. I told myself I was going to get a couple more hours of sleep and then I'd get up to make some moves with Heavy.

CHAPTER FOURTEEN

ISIS

I didn't know what had gotten into Quay, but he came in the house early and told me to get dressed. I'd been sitting on the couch watching TV, but I immediately got my ass up. The only times I went out lately were for doctor's appointments and when I snuck out to work my store, so I was all for leaving the house. I tried to ask what I should wear and all he told me was to show the fuck out. That just let me know it was going to be somewhere nice. Even though I'd already bathed when I first got up and hadn't done anything all day, I took a quick shower. It wasn't until I went to pick out something to wear that I realized I didn't have any dress up clothes in my new size. Damn near overnight the baby had grown so much that I could only see the toes of my feet unless I leaned forward. Everything that I'd gotten when Quay took me shopping was loungewear, and while I could dress almost anything up, I didn't want to. It had been a long time since I'd gotten sexy and I really wanted to blow his mind, but sweats or leggings wasn't the way. Eyeing my old clothes, I tried to find a dress that was formfitting but stretchy enough for me to squeeze into it. I narrowed it down to three dresses, and after a call to Adore I ended up going with the nude, mock neck one. It was nice and snug but I didn't feel uncomfortable or restricted. Since it came down to just below my knees, I paired it with some nude booties and accessorized with my gold Rolex, a simple gold cross, and gold spiral drop earrings.

Instead of trying to do too much with my hair, I put it in a high ponytail with curls, two bangs, and a few curly tendrils along the back and sides. The look was giving YSL Libre, so I sprayed some on my pressure points and layered it with Kay Ali Vanilla 28. After putting on some makeup, I began applying my Stunna Fenty lipstick when Quay appeared in the doorway.

"Damn, you got me ready to say fuck dinner, on my life!" His eyes lit up taking me in, and I couldn't help but beam from the compliment. He looked good as fuck too, dressed in all black from head to toe, with his ears, neck, and wrist shining. I'd never seen him so dressed up and I hoped he did it more often.

"Awww, thanks baby! You look good too," I gushed, turning around to face him. He zeroed in on my belly and immediately closed the short distance between us, rubbing it through my dress.

"You tryna throw that lil' pussy at me Ice?" He looked down at me, flashing all thirty-two teeth, but I was already shaking my head.

"Nope, I'm tryna go outside like you said." Folding my arms, I narrowed my eyes on his ass, making him crack the fuck up.

"I'm just fuckin' with you bae." He lifted my chin, pecking my lips softly. "It's time to go anyway 'cause we got reservations and I ain't tryna have you walkin' around in them heels for too long." Rolling my eyes at his slick comment, I left the bathroom to get the brown teddy bear trench coat I'd planned to wear. He was right behind me ready to help me slip it on, and smirked when he realized I couldn't close it.

"Don't even," I warned playfully. "It ain't my fault this baby stretching me out, asshole."

Shrugging, he threw his hands up with a laugh. "Ayyye, the bigger the better, that just means he's healthy." He was definitely in rare form but I didn't even mind. It had been a while since he'd been in such a consistently good mood and I'd really missed it. Clasping my hand in his, we headed downstairs and out to the truck. I was glad he had the foresight to start it because it was pretty cold out. I smiled on the inside when he opened my door for me and helped me into the passenger seat. Once he climbed in as well we pulled off and I quickly connected my phone to the Bluetooth.

"Don't be cutting on none of that he-man, nigga hating ass shit, Ice," he warned, mugging me, but I waved him off.

"Boy boom, I got this. I'm bouta set the mood." I could feel him eyeing me as I searched for the perfect song, and I instantly grinned when I found it.

If them bitches 'round you, better be blood
If it ain't me or your mama, shouldn't
Be showin' you no love
Please forgive me, I know that I'm stingy
'Cause baby, I'm gang 'bout you
Ain't playin' no games 'bout you
I'll go to hell or jail 'bout you boy
I'll go to hell or jail 'bout you boy

The sounds of Summer Walker and Jhene' Aiko's song "I'll Kill You" began blasting through the car and I instantly started singing along. It took him a minute to realize what she was saying because Summer Walker said stuff funny sometimes, but when he caught on he reached to snatch my phone. Still singing, I held it away from him as I danced in my seat.

"Maaaan—"

That's on my mama, yeah that's on the hood
Don't want no problems, I wish a bitch would
Try to come between us, it won't end up good

"Yo' ass got jokes!" he shouted over the music with a grin, no longer attempting to take my phone, and I happily continued singing until the next song on my playlist started. By the time he pulled over he'd began vibing too, while I scoped out the building he'd stopped at. I couldn't lie, I was impressed seeing the caliber of restaurant he'd chosen. Just from the outside I could tell it was a fancy one, and my excitement grew. I was so engrossed in my inspection I didn't even notice the valet that had come over until Quay opened my car door and reached for my hand.

"Oh my gosh, Quay! How'd you find out about this place?" I asked, stepping out next to him on the sidewalk as a doorman held open the door for us.

"Heavy put me on, but don't be actin' like I ain't never took yo' goofy ass nowhere nice before."

"I meeeeaan, The Cheesecake Factory cool, but it ain't *this*."

"You hell, man." He chuckled, shaking his head as we walked inside.

"Hello, welcome to Prosecco. Do you have a reservation?" the bubbly white hostess greeted us smiling extra hard and letting her eyes linger on Quay a few seconds too long. I wasn't even pressed though, he did look fine as hell. Instead, I flipped my coat back and put my hand on my hip, giving her a clear view of my belly.

"Yeah, under Wallace," Quay said. Already peeping what I was on, he wrapped his arms around me and kissed my cheek. She was so focused on the action that she froze, briefly forgetting what she was supposed to do with the information he'd given her. "You gone check that or some shit?" he eventually asked, and she jumped to attention, laughing awkwardly.

"Oh, sorry about that! Yes, we have you right here!" Her cheeks flamed red as she grabbed us some menus and led us through the restaurant. When we walked past the full bar and at least three empty tables, I glanced back at Quay quizzically. I was hoping her ass ain't try to put us in the back of the restaurant on some hating shit, because I was going to curse her the fuck out. She kept moving though, until we reached a private room and she pulled the curtains back. There was a table in the center of the room draped in a white tablecloth with a single candle on top.

Quay slipped behind me and helped me out of my coat before pulling out my chair for me like a real gentleman, and I swooned. The hostess, whose nametag read Hannah, handed us each a menu and let us know our waitress would be in shortly. Excusing herself, she left and it wasn't long when a waiter came in.

"Hi, I'm Terry and I'll be your waiter for the evening. Can I start you off with some wine?" he asked, looking from me to Quay with a smile, and I lifted a perfectly arched brow.

"Nah, don't even think about it." Quay instantly shook his head, making me pout.

"I can have a glass of red a day, it's good for the baby."

"Yeah ayite, you ain't bouta turn my baby into a lush. If it makes you feel better though, I won't have a drink either. Y'all got nonalcoholic champagne?" he asked, looking pleased when Terry said they did. "Bet, let us get two glasses of that."

Nodding, he scurried off to get our drinks, and I rolled my eyes as soon as he was gone. "Hater," I chided, finally looking at the menu to see what comfort food I could get in place of a light buzz. By the time Terry returned with our drinks, I'd already decided on the rack of lamb with the roasted fingerling potatoes and charred green beans. Quay ordered some type of chicken dish that came with spinach, adding the pasta with Italian sausage. I already knew exactly what he was on with his picky eating, but I didn't tease him about it, I just took a sip of my fake drink. Surprisingly it wasn't bad, it just tasted like sparkling water. After swallowing a bit, Quay's mouth twisted in dislike and I bit back a laugh at how childish he looked.

"That shit nasty as hell! How you even drinkin' it with a straight face?"

"It tastes like juice to me." I shrugged.

"Yeah, yo' ass crazy, 'cause that shit disgusting. Shit, it done left a nasty ass taste in my mouth." Gagging dramatically, he slid his glass over to me. "Here, you can have mine too so it won't go to waste." I was dying laughing at his cheap ass by now, but I still accepted the drink. The rest of the dinner went off without a hitch despite his lying ass ordering some actual alcohol, but I wasn't even tripping. We were in a good spot and I wasn't going to waste my time over the little things, I was just going to enjoy the moment.

CHAPTER FIFTEEN
ADORE

My baby's birthday was coming up and even though I was sure De'Niko wouldn't allow me to be at her party, I was still going to try to do something special for her on my own. I wanted to throw her a party also, but our visits were going so well I didn't want to rock the boat by asking for more than the judge had already given. Soon, there wouldn't be any limits to my access to her, as long as her father didn't get on bullshit.

"Did you see this one, Adore? You said she likes making things, right?" my mama asked, lifting a little friendship bracelet kit off the shelf. We were currently walking around Walmart and spending money I didn't need to spend, but that's how it always was when I went. Today was special though, so I didn't mind going a little overboard for my baby girl.

"Aw yeah, that is cute," I told her, adding it to the cart full of other stuff I had. I'd already gotten a couple outfits, some L.O.L Dolls, board games, and I even splurged on an iPhone for her with multiple phone cases. Unbeknownst to

De'Niko, she'd been dropping hints about wanting a phone. I honestly didn't see an issue with it, but as strict as the Blacks seemed when it came to her, I figured they probably wouldn't like it. All I knew was they better not try and take it from her.

"I'm still salty we can't throw our own party for her," my mama sighed. She'd been throwing little comments out here and there about Kaliyah's birthday and I honestly felt bad. Even though I had been telling my baby all about her grandma and uncle, I knew they couldn't wait to be free to actually spend time with her too, and vice versa. Kaliyah had mentioned how cool it would be to have another grandma already, so I knew she was going to be happy when they finally got together. From what I'd seen of De'Niko's mama, I knew she couldn't be that much fun, with her evil ass.

"Yeah, I know Ma, but this is only temporary and if it makes you feel better, we can do something special for her later on down the line."

"I just can't wait until this is all over." Grumbling, she adjusted her purse on her shoulder and continued to look over the other activity boxes on the shelves.

"Tell me about it," I agreed, looking off to the side, and my brows immediately dipped as I locked eyes with Farrah. She looked completely out of place dressed to the nines in designer from head to toe and what seemed like every piece of jewelry she owned. Crazy bitch didn't even have a cart.

"Is that who I think it is?" my mama quizzed from behind me, and I nodded with a hum.

"Mmmhmm."

"Chile, she look like she just stepped out an episode of *Dynasty*," she cracked, and I burst into laughter as Farrah headed in our direction. I had to admit that she was very pretty, and if she wasn't complicit in the bullshit going on with her in-laws I probably would've liked her, then again, that was a lie. She was way too stiff for me.

"Farrah, it's funny seeing you here." I smiled sweetly like I wasn't imagining hitting her ass with my cart. Her smile matched mine so I knew she was probably thinking something just as sinister as she eyed me up and down.

"Actually, it's not. I heard you were going to be picking up some things for Kaliyah's birthday and figured you'd come somewhere like this." She looked around, wrinkling her nose as if she wasn't talking about an eight-year-old. Regardless of the front she was putting on, I could smell the insecurity all over her and it almost had me feeling bad for her.

"Oh, is that right?" I hummed, shifting my weight to my other foot. "Well, is there something you want or did you just decide to come slum it for nothing?"

"Straight to the point, I can respect it. I'm gonna need you to respect my role as the first and only mother that Kaliyah knows as well though. It's cute that you're building your relationship and trying to win her over with this basic shit." She motioned over my cart with a wiggle of her fingers. "Don't think that a couple months of spoiling will just erase the impact that I've made as her mother over the last eight years." It was obvious she was trying to bait me with the bullshit she was talking, but all it did was cause a rumbling laugh to erupt from deep within my belly. The evil smirk she wore immediately fell off her face, and she took a step back like I was insane.

"Girl, go to hell!" I cackled and then stopped, abruptly moving around my cart so I could get right in her face. The move had her looking to my mama like she could save her, but that was a dead issue. If anything, my mama was going to be the first to swing. "I don't know what De'Niko and his lying ass family told you to make you feel so bold, honey, but they basically stole my baby and kept her away from me for those eight years. You may have stepped up to help raise her, but be clear, Kaliyah is *my* daughter and nothing you say or do is going to change that. Now if you'll excuse me, I have to finish *spoiling* my baby. You know you only turn nine once." Pulling my cart behind me, I made sure to shoulder bump her ass hard enough that she stumbled in the kitten heels she wore.

"Giiiiirl, you got way more self-control than me! I had to hold on to the cart so I wouldn't slap the shit outta her," my mama said, shaking her head as we turned down another aisle, and I chuckled.

"Tuh, I'm not bouta let her hatin' ass mess up me gettin' custody of my baby. She gone have to come harder than that."

"She still needs her ass beat, so I'ma put her down for one as soon as all this shit over with," she said so nonchalantly that I had to laugh. My mama was just crazy enough to do something like have a list for people she was going to beat up. I was almost positive it was a tie for the top spot between my daddy and De'Niko Sr. One thing she didn't play about was her kids.

After leaving my mama, I spent hours wrapping up each of Kaliyah's gifts, and by the time I was finished Heavy was coming through the door looking tired as hell. Kay Kay was laid out over his shoulder and after stopping to give me a quick kiss, he went to put her to bed while I cleaned up my mess. Looking at the pile of presents, I had to admit I'd gone slightly overboard, but I couldn't wait to see the look on her face when she saw them. I actually had one other gift that I needed to pick up for her and it was really special to me. I'd ordered us both heart necklaces that were being inscribed. Just thinking about being able to give them to her had me excited as hell, even though we still had about a week and a half before her birthday.

When I made it upstairs, Heavy was at the dresser getting some clothes for bed. I laid my head on his back and hugged him from behind, relishing in my happiness. He'd made my life so much better since coming into it, and sometimes it was hard to believe he was mine. "What's up? You straight?" he asked, twisting his neck so he could look down at me.

"Yeah, I just missed you," I murmured and held him tighter. Even after a long day, he smelled just as heavenly as he had when he'd left that morning. I was over-addicted to every-thing about him, down to the way he felt in my arms. His laughter had his body vibrating against mine, even though I was dead serious.

"I missed you too, shorty." Grabbing one of my hands, he gave a little tug and pulled me around in front of him. He bent down, pressing a kiss to my lips, and I shivered a little from the contact. "Come take a shower with me." He nodded toward the bathroom where the shower was already running.

After a quickie that had my knees weak, we both washed up and laid down for the night. I fell asleep on his chest like I'd been doing since moving in with him, feeling thankful that God had blessed me the way he did after everything I'd gone through.

CHAPTER SIXTEEN
HEAVY

My mama's words had been weighing heavy on me for the last couple weeks and even though I didn't feel like it was the best decision, I was ready to finally take Kay Kay to see her mama. I climbed out of bed seeing that Adore was already up and went to handle my hygiene. After throwing on a black thermal, some dark jeans, and my black Timbs, I squirted on a little cologne and was ready for the day. When I made it downstairs, Kay Kay and Adore were at the table eating bowls of cereal.

"How's two of my favorite girl's doin'?" I asked, giving them each a kiss before dropping into a chair and pouring myself a bowl of Cinnamon Toast Crunch.

"Adore had a nightmare!" Kay Kay's bad ass was thirsty to say. Kids were crazy like that, because it was obvious judging from the look on Adore's face that she didn't want to talk about it, even though Kay Kay seemed excited. Frowning, I took in her demeanor and noted how off she seemed, just staring into space while holding onto the necklace she shared with Kaliyah.

"Aye, you straight?" I touched her arm lightly to get her attention and she jumped.

"Huh? Oh, yeah, I'm cool. Just a little weirded out." Shrugging, she resumed eating but when she noticed me still watching her, she rolled her eyes and forced out a giggle. "Seriously, I'm good, Dominique. Nightmares always have me a little off. I'll be fine by the time I get to work." Deciding to drop it for now, I nodded and finished my cereal.

"Well, since it's no school can I ditch dance today too?" Kay Kay looked over at me, face lit up with hopefulness. She didn't know it but I'd already planned on taking her to see Sha'ron, and I wasn't sure if she'd even want to go to dance after that anyway.

"Uh yeah, I was actually gonna take you to see yo' mom today anyway, soo..." My voice trailed off as she cheered, clapping her hands together happily. It made me feel even worse for taking so long, but at the same I knew her mood was going to change as soon as she was made privy to the situation.

"Yess! I can show her my new bracelet! I'm bouta go get dressed!" She ran off, ponytails bouncing behind her. I was glad my OG had braided her up for me so I'd have a couple of weeks without having to worry about it. I could feel Adore's eyes on me, and when I faced her she looked sympathetic.

"When did you decide this?" she asked, covering my hand with hers, and I shrugged.

"My OG decided for me, but to be honest, it's time. It don't look like she's comin' outta this, and I don't wanna be the reason Kay Kay doesn't get to say goodbye." It hurt having to say that shit out loud. Sha'ron should've still been around to see our daughter graduate and get married and shit, so to know that she probably wasn't going to be able to do those things because of De'Niko Black had me pissed off. I was moving slow with my plan, but he was definitely going to get his for the shit he'd done.

"I'm sorry, babe. I don't know Sha'ron but nobody deserves nothing like this happening to them, and I can't help but feel like it's partly my fault. De'Niko would've never had a reason to do that if it wasn't for you helping me out. It seems like every time I turn around my decisions effect somebody else." I was already shaking my head.

"Nah, don't do that." I frowned. I didn't want her blaming herself for how fucked up my pops was, and I realized I'd probably have to tell her the truth soon. "This ain't got nothin' to do with you. His old ass did that goofy shit on his own, and it wasn't for nothin' 'cause it still ain't stop shit around here, and it won't. I'm *not* goin' nowhere," I promised, leaning onto the table and enclosing her hand in mine. She nodded, misty eyed, but I could tell my words didn't help her to feel any better.

"Look, I'ma be honest with you, ayite. Black already got a vendetta against me 'cause—"

"I'm ready, Daddy!" Kay Kay came rushing back into the kitchen, now dressed in a pair of colorful leggings and a white tee with the same design on the sleeves. I immediately straightened, covering up the awkward moment by clearing my throat while Adore wiped her face.

"Ayite, let's roll, baby girl." I tried to distract her so she wouldn't notice the tension, and thankfully she was so engrossed in packing her things into her little purse that she paid us no attention. "We'll finish this later, ayite. I really don't know how long we gone be but—"

"It's cool babe, I need to get to the restaurant anyway." She gave me a quick kiss and rushed out the kitchen after saying goodbye to Kay Kay. Sighing, I watched her until she disappeared around the corner and cursed inwardly. I didn't have time to worry about it at the moment though, because I still needed to explain shit to Kay Kay before we made it to the hospital.

After an extremely uncomfortable ride, where I told my daughter the least traumatizing version of what happened to her mother, we pulled up to the hospital in silence. She sat still staring out the window, unmoving as the car came to a stop.

"Alright, you ready baby?" I finally asked, looking at her in the rearview. I wasn't ready to walk my baby in there to her worst nightmare. Seeing her hurt and not being able to fix it was already the worst thing I could think of, and now it was coming true. She nodded silently, and I climbed out, coming around to open the door for her. Holding my hand tightly, we rode up to her mother's room only to find Sandra's ass sitting in there. She immediately turned up her nose at the sight of me. The look I gave let her know to keep her cool with my shorty around and she took heed, forcing a smile on her face.

"Hey sweetie! You've gotten so big! Come on over here and give yo' granny a hug." Kay Kay slowly released my hand but instead of going over to her, she detoured to her mother's side. Sandra's bitch ass didn't like that shit and sat back twisting her lips, but she made sure to keep them closed. I stood off to the side, taking my eyes off her long enough to see Kay Kay's quiet tears hitting her cheeks. Time had allowed some of the bruising and swelling to go away so she didn't look as bad as before, but I was sure it still fucked our daughter up.

"Is she gonna die, Daddy?" she finally asked, looking over at me fearfully. Sandra gasped, covering her mouth while I fought back tears. My voice cracked and I pinched the bridge of my nose to keep myself from crying.

"I-I don't know, Kay Kay. I hope not." I swallowed hard, focusing on the slow rise and fall of Sha'ron's chest. I wasn't scared of shit, no man, no weapon, not even the thought of death put fear in my heart, but it terrified me to look into my baby's face right then.

"She's going to be just fine, don't you even worry about that," Sandra interjected, and my jaw twitched. The last thing I wanted was for Kay Kay to get false hope, especially when it was looking like the complete opposite was going to happen. Instead of disagreeing with her and starting a whole argument, I took the only other chair in the room.

We ended up staying there for over an hour, and after a while Kay Kay relaxed and was able to end the visit in a better mood than when we arrived. Sandra was still there when we left, promising to pick Kay Kay up the next day. Since my baby seemed like she wanted to go, I didn't put up a fight. However, if anything happened to my child in her care, she already knew what she'd get.

Once we were back in the car and heading home, I took a detour instead, taking her to grab a bite to eat. I felt like I needed a minute alone with her to find out where her head was at since she'd been so quiet. As her father I felt it necessary to have a conversation with her about what she'd seen and how she felt. I pulled into a McDonald's and she didn't even seem happy like she usually did.

"You wanna talk about yo' mama?" I asked once we were seated with our food, and she shrugged innocently. "You can ask me anything you want." Sure, she'd asked me questions on the way to the hospital and I'd answered to the best of my ability, but hearing about something and seeing something with your own eyes were two different things.

"Since the police don't know who did it, can the person come get us?" She bit into her burger and chewed thoughtfully. I hated that she was worrying about our safety. There wasn't shit she needed to worry about and I made sure I told her that.

"You're perfectly safe, baby girl. Nobody's gonna hurt

either one of us," I promised, studying her face, and she visibly relaxed.

"Okay." She nodded and continued eating silently. I assumed my answer satisfied her curiosity because she didn't ask anything else and I didn't push, but this was just another reason I needed to handle Black ASAP.

CHAPTER SEVENTEEN

QUAY

Shit at home had been much better since I took Isis out to dinner, and I had to admit it was a weight off my shoulder. Her hardheaded ass was doing what she was supposed to and my baby was growing every day. Just like I imagined, she looked good all big and pregnant. Seeing my baby growing inside of her was the sexiest shit I'd ever seen and I realized, I wasn't even looking at other bitches the same. That was wild for me because I was always looking for the next best thing even when I knew I wanted to be with her. It was just something about new pussy that was alluring as fuck, but I knew what I had at the crib. Even when I found myself looking too long, Isis's face was the first thing that popped into my head, stopping shit before it even got started. That was some growth for me, and it felt good.

"What you lookin' at like that?" Isis huffed, waddling around the kitchen, and I realized I'd been staring at her again.

"Shiiiit, just thinking about taking you upstairs and eatin' yo' pussy." I smirked and licked my lips real slow, sending her into a fit of giggles.

"Well, that's gone be kinda hard to do since we got a doctor's appointment in about thirty minutes."

Just that quick I'd forgotten about her appointment. Even though she was doing well, she was still going every week and I didn't play about that shit. "Shit, that's cool, I'ma just get you when we come home." Shrugging, I got up from the table as she continued eating her grapes with a laugh.

"I'm taking a nap when we get back sir, but you're more than welcome to join me."

"Nap my ass," I grumbled, already shaking my head as I rubbed her stomach, and my son instantly balled up where my hand was. It was like he knew when I was close and touching him because he always moved or kicked whenever I put my hands on him. "What's up son, you ready to bust up outta there, huh?" I bent and spoke straight to him, before placing her a kiss on her well-oiled skin.

"Quay stooooop! It hurts when he does that!" Bumping me out the way, she began rubbing her stomach to try and make him straighten out like I'd seen her do a lot lately. I couldn't help the smile that slid across my face watching her as she pouted. She was in a pair of pink sweatpants and the cropped matching hoodie, with her hair in a sloppy bun that was flopping around every time she moved her head. She wasn't even trying that hard and I knew she'd be shitting on every woman we'd see.

"My bad, let me help you out." Replacing her hand with mine, I rubbed from the top to the bottom until he eventually straightened himself out and relief washed over her face. Once she was good I dropped a quick kiss on her lips. "Ayite, let's go. The faster I get you home the faster we can take a *nap*." My exaggeration of the word had her laughing again as she pushed me away from her so she could finish getting ready, even though I was dead ass serious.

Not even an hour later we were headed back home from her appointment, and if it wasn't for my son I'd be complaining about having to take these short ass trips. Just like the week before everything was good, both Isis and the baby were right on track and she was now twenty-one weeks. That meant I was almost eighteen weeks away from being able to hold my little man, and I couldn't wait. The thought had me cheesing to myself as I drove.

"You think we can stop by the store and do the inventory since we haven't gotten it done?" Isis mused from the passenger seat. I can't lie, I had been putting it off for a minute because I didn't want her doing anything strenuous that could've set her back, but I was in such a good mood I agreed.

"Yeah, I got you," I sighed, hoping that the back of the truck would be enough room for whatever she had. It wasn't too far away from where we were so I took a quick detour and pulled up in front of the store about ten minutes later. Getting out, I went around and helped Isis down onto the sidewalk and followed behind her up to the door. She quickly let us in and I immediately noticed how bare the sales floor was looking when she flipped on the lights. "You sure ain't nobody been in this muhfucka since you been home?" I frowned, looking around as she waddled toward the back.

"You know damn well it wouldn't look this good if I got robbed." She read my mind with a scoff, beckoning me further. "Come on, everything in the back." Still confused as fuck, I followed her into her storage room where there were boxes everywhere. I knew for damn sure all of it wouldn't fit today, but I'd take as much as I could and figure out something for the rest.

"Tell me what you need the most and we'll take that now, 'cause all this shit ain't gone fit in the back," I told her, hiking up my jeans as she poked out her lips and looked at each of the boxes.

"Okay, definitely all these ones over here. That's winter stuff." She pointed. "Annnnd maybe a couple of these too." I already knew I was gone fuck around and be sweating by the time I was done, but I got right to work carrying two boxes at a time. The first group of boxes she'd told me to get easily fit into the truck, and after dropping the backseat I was able to fit in six more with a little struggle. I was making my last trip back inside to get Isis, and my face balled up at the sight of two bitches inside looking through the racks and my baby mama nowhere in sight.

"Aye, what the fuck y'all doin'? We ain't open!" Both women immediately jumped at the sound of my voice and shared a look.

"Umm, the lights on though." The one furthest away from me motioned over her head with her nose turned up.

"But it ain't the open sign," I said, speaking slowly so her dumb ass would understand. "Look, we only here picking up inventory so she can open an online store, but right now ain't shit for sale." I wasn't trying to be rude, but I also wasn't trying to stay any longer than I had to. Sucking their teeth, they both slammed their items back on the racks and switched out, talking shit under their breaths.

"I ain't comin' up here no more! Her hours been too fucked up this last month! Ain't nobody got time to be checking to see if she open every day!"

"Girl, I swear, her ass was just open this same time last week so I don't know what the fuck going on." My eyes immediately narrowed when she said that, and I caught her by the arm before she could make it all the way out the door. "Hey—"

"What you just say? This store was open last week?" I asked for clarification, because I just knew her ass was lying. I damn sure hadn't brought Isis up to the store, and since she didn't have an assistant then it had to have been her lying ass up there.

"Yeah," she snorted. "Isis been opening up for a couple hours every day, it's just random hours. Sometimes it's in the morning and sometimes it's in the afternoon or evening," she said nastily, and my jaw clenched angrily as I damn near shoved her ass out the door. I needed to get myself together before I went back into the storage room with Isis or else I was going to choke her dumbass out. She thought she was real smart sneaking her ass up there whenever I'd leave the house, and I hadn't suspected shit.

When I felt like I'd calmed down enough, I stalked to the back where Isis was sitting in a swivel chair and rubbing her belly. Her face lit up when she saw me and she immediately reached out so I could help her up. Instead of pulling her to her feet though, I dropped into the chair across from her and slid it until I was right in front of her lying ass.

"You still been runnin' the store," I grit, and it came out as more of a statement than a question. The amused bewilderment on her face quickly dropped to straight bewilderment as she prepared to lie.

"No, I—"

"*Don't* fuckin' lie, Ice." Her eyes immediately began to water, and her lips quivered as she held her stomach defensively. I just held her gaze, unmoved, waiting for her to admit that she'd lied and put my baby in danger, for I didn't even know what. I could only assume it was just to defy me because even when I was my maddest at her, I was still providing. She didn't want for shit, and my only demand was that she did what the fuck the doctor told her to. It wasn't enough that she'd already killed one of my babies, but now she was risking my son as well. I just couldn't even believe this shit.

"I never stay long. I-I don't even stand up while I'm here and I—" She was getting more and more worked up despite how calm I was, and I realized I wasn't even as mad as I was disappointed.

"Why? Huh? Why the fuck would you risk our baby's life just to come up in here? It ain't like I didn't give you money, you got a place to stay, so why the fuck was this shit necessary?" I really needed to know. I needed this shit to make sense to me.

"I don't know. I guess I just didn't want to be financially dependent on you, but you know that's how I am, Quay. That's not the way my mama raised me. I can't just depend on a nigga's word 'cause—"

"So now you can't depend on me? Since we been fuckin' around I been givin' you more than just my fuckin' word! You got my time, my support, shit, you holdin' my future, and yo' ass willin' to throw all this shit away for a few extra dollars!" She'd broken out into a full-blown sob by now, but I wasn't moved at all and was glad for the distraction of my phone going off. Of course, when it rained it fucking poured. Hector wanted to see Heavy and me ASAP. "Look, we gotta go, I got some shit to do," I told her much more calmly, and she blinked rapidly, looking up at me shocked.

"So that's it, we're not gonna finish talking about this?" she gasped, and I ran my hand over my head, avoiding her eyes.

"It ain't shit else to talk about. Come on so I can drop you off," I told her dryly, helping her out of the chair. Not wanting to let shit go, she continued to huff and puff as she made her way from the back and out onto her sales floor. She quickly realized that I was checked the fuck out though, and after locking up I wasted no time taking her ass home. I'd have to deal with her later.

CHAPTER EIGHTEEN
ISIS

I t had been two weeks since Quay found out about me still running my store and he hadn't said more than two words to me. Not that he was home very often anyway to say shit. He was leaving early and coming in late, probably not even getting a full four hours of sleep before he was back out on the streets again. It was like he was only coming home to change clothes and make sure I was still alive. I couldn't lie, I was sick. I'd let my mama's teachings have me risking my health, when the truth was that Quay would've never let my store close.

Resting on my side, I rubbed the spot where the baby was stretching and he immediately started to kick, making me smile despite my sadness. Since Quay had been unavailable, I'd been buying up all types of baby stuff online and the boxes were piling up by the door. He'd hired Rex to keep an eye on me for the remainder of my pregnancy since he was no longer trailing Adore, but when he asked about the packages, I only told him to stack them in the living room. I wanted to set up the baby's room with Quay, and I figured if he saw all the stuff

I'd gotten he'd get in daddy mode and it would be a bonding experience. Unfortunately, he ignored that shit like he was ignoring me. Even for my last appointment, Rex had taken me and he'd met us up there like a real dick. I understood that I'd fucked up, but it hurt my feelings how quickly he was able to shut down on me and our baby. Just a couple of weeks ago he couldn't keep his hands off my belly, and now he didn't even look my way.

"Hey, I made grilled cheese and soup." Ms. Pam entered the room with a food tray and I almost laughed. She'd also been staying with me when she could, and although she was good company, she wasn't my damn baby daddy.

"Ma, not you feedin' me this lil' middle school lunch," I huffed, sitting up so she could sit the try over my lap. "I really ain't had this in I don't know how long."

"First of all, I like grilled cheese and soup, and second of all, it ain't nobody fault you ain't had none in a while." Shrugging, she got comfortable next to me and grabbed one of the buttery sandwiches, taking a big bite. I couldn't stunt, it did look good and my stomach growled loudly. Ms. Pam didn't say shit as she looked at me with a raised brow, still chewing her own food. Lifting one of the triangular pieces, I dipped it in the soup before taking a bite. It was buttery and soft, basically melting in my mouth, and I had to glance over at Ms. Pam, impressed.

"Okay yeah, this is fye!" I admitted, nodding as I continued eating up every sandwich in front of me besides two so that M. Pam would have some.

"Oh, I know." She winked and changed the subject. "So do you want me to help you start putting together some of that stuff you got piled up at the door, or did Quay already say he was gonna do it?" she asked after a while, and my eyes instantly dropped. I hadn't really said anything about what was going on, but I knew he had told her *something* about it.

After the last time, he never wanted to put her and Adore too far into our business 'cause he didn't want them cursing him out. It figured.

"Yeah, he's supposed to be doing it soon," I lied, knowing damn well he hadn't said shit to me about those boxes. He was so far removed he probably didn't even know what was in that shit. I understood him being upset, but the way he was ignoring my baby was childish.

"Oh, well okay. I'll say something to him about it, and if he doesn't do it then I'm here with nothing to do but stress about my grandbaby's arrival." Chuckling, she finished eating and went to take the tray down to the kitchen. As soon as she was gone I laid back down, trying to will myself not to cry at how fucked up shit was. It should've been no reason for the nigga I lived with to be informed of something at our house by his mama. I didn't like the way he was moving, but I also couldn't blame anyone but myself. That didn't stop it from hurting though.

I must have fallen asleep when she left because the next thing I knew it was dark outside. The sound of thumping in the other room had me on high alert, and I checked the time to see it was almost one in the morning. Squinting, I listened harder as my heart pounded and realization hit me. "I just know damn well this nigga ain't," I growled, throwing my feet over the side of the bed. It was much harder to move fast with my belly in the way, but once I'd slipped on my house shoes and stood up, I looked around for something to beat his ass with.

My umbrella was the first thing my eyes landed on and I quickly lifted it over my shoulder, hoping I didn't break it before I got a chance to physically harm my baby daddy. Sticking my head out into the hallway, I was able to actually hear voices even though they weren't too loud. I felt slightly relieved that they weren't coming from the master bedroom, so as disrespectful as he was, he wasn't fucking some random in the bed we shared. In the opposite direction was his other guest room and I slowly made my way to the door, pausing long enough to listen. The low rumble of my nigga's voice sounded and then a girl's loud ass giggle came next. That was all it took for me to burst inside with my umbrella over my head.

"You dirty muthafucka!" I screamed, expecting to find Quay fucking some hoe. Instead, he was on the floor shirtless, surrounded by the pieces to what looked like the changing table I'd bought. He looked at me with his face twisted irritably before picking up his phone and silencing the video he was watching.

"Take yo' paranoid ass back to bed, Ice," he sneered, putting his red eyes back on the piece he was working on. Feeling stupid, I backed out of the room and returned to bed with tears streaking my face. At this point, I didn't even know what I was crying for. The fact that he looked so adorable sitting up putting the baby's bedroom together or because my damn feelings were hurt from him yelling at me. I couldn't help feeling like I'd singlehandedly ruined our good stretch we were on, and I didn't know how we'd be able to come back from this. Closing the door behind me so that he wouldn't hear me ugly crying, I climbed back in bed and held my pillow against my chest, eventually crying myself to sleep.

When I woke up a few hours later, he was gone and I rolled my eyes. The only good thing was that when I peeked into the guestroom, I saw that he'd completed the changing table and the crib and had them in place against opposite walls. I'd gone with a silver theme and planned to make the room light blue and dark blue with silver accents. The way shit was going though, I'd probably need to be finding my own place once again and just decorating it there.

After checking out the room, I handled my hygiene and got dressed in some leggings and a graphic tee. Piling my hair on top of my head, I grabbed my laptop and went to work finding somebody to start my website because I didn't know what I was doing. Once I got in touch with a web designer and gave them the details of what I wanted the site to consist of, I headed down to the basement where Quay had taken all my boxes. It ended up taking hours to sort and count my inventory, but I definitely had more than enough to carry me through the winter from home.

When I finally dragged myself back upstairs, I made myself a snack that was more like a meal and while I ate I ordered a couple of things to be delivered. I put a rush on my order for custom shipping packages so that when the lady Virginia finally finished my website I'd be able to start receiving orders right away. I ended up looking up promotional items when a Facetime call came through from Adore. "Hey boo."

"Heeey, don't you look all pretty and shit! My nephew got you over there glowing, girl!" she cheesed, putting her face all in the camera, and I rolled my eyes. The very last thing I was feeling was glowy or pretty, especially considering that I hadn't done shit but wash my face and barely brushed my hair.

"Yeah ayite, you're the one looking like you got on some Body Lava from Fenty. You sure I ain't got another lil' niece or nephew comin'?" I was joking, but I wasn't at the same time. There was a chance that Heavy and her visits with Kaliyah had a lot to do with her glow, but I kind of had my fingers crossed for another baby too.

"Why you keep sayin' that?" She frowned, pushing her lips into an exaggerated pout. "Besides, a baby would only make stuff worse at the moment."

"Hold up, what you mean by worse? I know Heavy ain't over there actin' up, is he?" Leaning forward, I prepared for her to tell me that we needed to fuck a nigga up. I'd slacked on my best friend duties last time, but I wasn't going to let that shit happen again. Her brows dipped in and she quickly shook her head.

"What! No, Heavy's been great, shit, everything's been great. It's almost time to go back to court to find out if I can get joint custody of Kaliyah. Ms. Pam has convinced me to take the manager position at the new restaurant since it'll be opening in the next month, and aside from Sha'ron being in the hospital everything is perfect. It's just...."

"Nah uh, don't do that, friend," I immediately chastised. I could already see where she was going with this, and I wasn't trying to hear it. "That's all good news and you deserve it babe."

"Yeah, but do I really?" My eyebrows rose at that because there was no reason for her to question whether or not she deserved her blessings. "I've been having nightmares." She lowered her voice like she didn't want anybody around her to hear.

"What you mean nightmares?" I was almost afraid to ask. The way she was talking sounded like the beginning of a scary movie. Looking around, she ducked closer to the screen.

"Bitch, you know, like nightmares about.... CiCi," she damn near whispered, and I sighed heavily. Since the shit with CiCi had happened, Adore hadn't said anything to me about being haunted. It was the general consensus that what happened was an accident, pushed to a tragedy by CiCi's ass. In my opinion, there wasn't shit for Adore to feel guilty about. She was trying to leave and I knew that for a fact because she'd called me. CiCi was the one that was fishing for a fight, and if she hadn't been trying to act hard then she would still be here to live another day. Just thinking about how she'd ruined my friend's life had me irritated.

"Girl, fuck her! She ain't got no right to be haunting you when she's the one that attacked you that day when you were pregnant! That could've very well been yo' ass dead because she was out here being dick dizzy—"

"I don't think *she's* haunting me, girl! I think I have survivor's remorse or some shit. Like somewhere in my mind I feel guilty about so much good shit happening to me when she's dead and gone," she cut me off and explained. And I immediately understood what she was saying, but I knew if that was the case then nothing I said would help her.

"Damn, you might need to talk to somebody because I can tell you till I'm blue in the face how much you deserve happiness after everything you've gone through, but obviously you're holding on to some type of guilt babe, and you shouldn't be." I felt bad seeing her eyes well up with tears at the truth to my words.

"Maybe after this next court hearing. The last thing I wanna do is give the judge a reason to think I'm not fit to be a part of my daughter's life."

"Damn, I didn't even think about that." I sighed, shaking my head. "You would think they want people to take care of their mental wellbeing, but I can definitely see De'Niko making a big deal about it in a negative way."

"Shit, I'll call you back later, my damn break is over already," she rushed. After saying our goodbyes, she hung up, but she was still on my mind for some time later. It was fucked up that so much of her life was controlled by somebody else and I knew I didn't want that for me and Quay. Even though he wasn't a court type of nigga, I still figured that sharing our son wasn't something I wanted to deal with and besides that, he deserved to see his parents together, and happily. I just needed to figure out a way to make that happen and soon.

CHAPTER NINETEEN
ADORE

I was surprised that Isis said I looked good because I hadn't been getting a lot of sleep at all. It had me feeling ran down and tired most of the time. I was having to drink energy drinks and multiple cups of coffee just to make it through the day without falling the fuck out. Heavy didn't even seem to notice since he was so tied up with helping Kay Kay deal with her mama and figuring out how to handle De'Niko. If he had noticed, he would've been the first to try and help me get over whatever I had going on, but I didn't want to take his attention away from those important tasks just for my mental bullshit.

"You ready?" Heavy's voice interrupted my thoughts, and I realized I was still sitting in front of the mirror in a zone.

"Oh yeah. I'll be right out." It was finally the day the judge would determine how we would move forward with Kaliyah's custody. Our visits had been going well, and I knew that when asked she'd definitely want to spend more than just a couple of hours a month with me. I nervously ran a hand over my hair that was silk pressed and unlocked the bathroom door, coming face to face with Heavy. "Oh shit!" I damn near jumped out of my skin, not having expected him to still be there.

"You straight?" He tilted his head, locking eyes with me.

"Y-yeah, you, uh, just scared me. I thought you left already." My voice was shaky, and I forced my eyes away from him, laughing nervously. The deflection did nothing to throw him off; in fact, it only seemed to make him more concerned. Cupping my chin, he forced me to look at him.

"Look, I know you're nervous but you don't have to ever hide anything from me, especially something like this. We're supposed to be each other's rocks and I can't be that for you if you don't allow me to be," he said, and it was like I felt every word he said in my soul. Nodding in agreement, I closed my eyes and took a cleansing breath. It wasn't really that I was nervous but more like sleep deprived, but again, that was a conversation I wasn't ready to have with him, especially right then.

"Thanks baby, I really do appreciate you," I told him, meaning it wholeheartedly.

"Good, 'cause I appreciate yo' ass too." Smiling, he broke the seriousness of the conversation, and this time my laugh wasn't forced at all. "That's what I'm tryna see. Now let's go get Kaliyah."

An hour later, Quay, my mama, Heavy, and I were led into the courtroom by my lawyer, where the Blacks were already sitting in a huddle. They immediately looked up at us with contempt, but I didn't let them shake me. My lawyer and the judge had already proven that they weren't untouchable and that really had me unbothered. Taking a seat, I listened while Lacy told me what all would happen today.

"I feel really good about this girl. You've done everything

the judge asked and Mr. Golds has nothing but great things to say about you, so this is definitely going to go off without a hitch," she beamed, giving my hand a squeeze.

"Thank you so much Lacy, I really don't know what I would do without you stepping up and helping me out."

"It's nothin'. The Blacks may scare a lot of attorneys, but they definitely don't put no fear in my heart." She rolled her eyes just as the bailiff came in and told us to rise for the judge. I focused my attention on Judge Howard, silently praying everything went well.

"Okay, let's get right to it. I've already spoken to the minor and I also have the reports from a Mr. Lee Golds, the supervisor for your visits, Adore. According to him, you've come on time for every visit and spent the entire time actually paying attention to the minor. You still have your position at the restaurant and are scheduled to get a promotion in the next month. I feel as though it only makes sense that you and Mr. and Mrs. Black begin a regular visitation schedule." She paused when gasps rang out around the courtroom, staring coldly over her reading glasses until it quieted back down. "Visitation will be overnight every other week, and Ms. Wallace will be given a schedule for the child's school and extracurricular activities. Congratulations." She banged the gavel, and I was already up screaming and hugging Lacy and my family.

"Wait, Your Honor, you can't expect that this will be in the child's best interest to bounce from home to home weekly. We haven't even had someone inspect her home!" De'Niko's lawyer stood up and tried to argue, even though the judge was already preparing to leave the courtroom. It was a desperate attempt, but I still froze, looking at the judge fearfully like she would change her mind just from his word.

"Counselor, I've banged my gavel and that means court is

over. I advise you to talk to your client and make sure they are prepared for the new arrangement." He stood there dumbfounded as she left the courtroom, and I could literally feel the heat coming from the Black family, but they were smart enough to just storm out of the courtroom with their tails tucked.

"You ready to answer a few questions?" Lacy asked as we all stood outside the double doors preparing to be swamped by the media, and I nodded confidently. I'd had a lot more practice when taking on the reporters. Half the time it didn't matter what I said anyway since the mayor and his lying ass family were the main ones under scrutiny.

Just like last time, the Blacks had scurried out of the building quickly and were nowhere in sight when we exited the courtroom. We only stuck around for about ten minutes before leaving ourselves for a celebratory lunch. Even as tired as I was, the excitement of being able to bring my daughter home was enough to keep me wide awake. When I got home though, I immediately took a nap.

After my win in court, I realized that I needed to take Isis's advice. It took me a couple of days to find the right therapist for me. I settled on an older Black woman, feeling confident that we could relate to each other better and she'd speak my language. I felt like it would be good to have my first session with her before I began my overnights with Kaliyah, and thankfully she had something open for the same day.

After checking in with the receptionist, I was advised to take a seat and I used the time to look around. The waiting area was well lit and decorated in nudes and tans with chocolate accents that somehow put me at ease. I liked that she scheduled her appointments so that her clients didn't run into each other while waiting. Not even ten minutes later, Dr. Jessica

Ports came out and I was mesmerized by how much prettier she was in person. She was a tall BBW, with blemish-free dark skin and a huge, glossy twist out.

"Adore?" She smiled, sticking her hand out to me, and I stood to accept it, noting how warm it was.

"Hi, that's me."

"Okay, well come on back. I'm glad you could make it." She led me into her office that was decorated similarly to the waiting room and closed the door behind us. Just like on TV, there was a couch and chair in the center of the room and her desk was tucked off in the corner. There were plants standing in corners and also hanging from the ceiling like a safari and a full wall bookcase full of books from top to bottom. "Have a seat, get comfortable." She pointed to the couch and I sat down awkwardly on the edge.

"Do I need to lay down or...?" I asked, and she shrugged, easing into her chair.

"Either is fine, whatever makes you more comfortable." I ended up just sitting with my hands clasped together between my thighs. "Okay, so what bring you in today?"

"Well, I, uhh. I've been having trouble sleeping. I keep having nightmares about someone from my past, someone I, uhh, wronged."

Her perfectly arched brows dipped. "Okay, so why don't you start from the beginning?" She held her pen poised, waiting for me to run down the whole story. I decided to explain the CiCi situation before anything since that's what I was currently having problems with. By the time I finished she'd filled the whole page of her notebook while I sat there nervously.

"So do you believe you're having these nightmares because of how well your life is going?" she finally asked, and I blew out a deep breath as tears burned my eyes. That was exactly what I'd been thinking and I hated how guilty I felt for simply living. Giving me a sympathetic look, she handed me a box of Kleenex and I dabbed at my eyes with a nod. "Mmhmm. I can understand that. You're getting your life back on track and it seems as though now you're being haunted, but I think it's actually more than just CiCi. I think you're holding on to a belief that you don't deserve all of the good things that's happening to you after suffering for so long. Why do you feel like you're undeserving of the life you're building after you've worked so hard to achieve it?" she posed, and I didn't know what to say. So many people had told me how deserving I was of happiness, but it was like I could never convince myself.

"I honestly don't know. I feel like no matter what I do, I won't be able to escape what I've done. Like no matter what I achieve, I'll still be the same old girl that got pregnant by an ain't shit nigga, except I messed around and took someone's life and went to prison."

"Okay, that's a lot to unpack. Yes, you were a teen mother; however, you were a child that was basically manipulated by an older man. And in his manipulation, you were brought into a messy situation that was not your fault. You were already stressed and emotional and completely blindsided by a violent woman you didn't even know. In an effort to protect yourself and your unborn child a terrible accident happened, but you should not be the only one that should take the blame for what happened." I felt everything that she said and received it, but it was only in this moment, and I would probably begin having my doubts once I was alone.

An alarm went off marking the end of the session, and Jessica leaned forward. "Saved by the bell," she said, making me chuckle at her joke. "I actually have an assignment for you to complete before next week. I want you to write down all of the reasons you believe you deserve the life you're building for yourself, and we'll go over it together." Feeling better, I headed out, stopping at the front desk to schedule my next appointment. I was happy to be working on myself and planned on continuing to make progress for myself.

CHAPTER TWENTY
HEAVY

Since Adore had been awarded joint custody, it was time to go through with my plans and a nigga was excited as hell. It was well past time for the Blacks to get what was coming to them and I was glad to be the one to bring it. The last twenty-four hours had been crazy after someone leaked a bunch of paperwork connecting the mayor and his son to none other than Hector. It had been a complete media mess, with the Blacks's pictures plastered on every news site and gossip blog. They were already talking about the amount of prison time they each would get for their crime.

Adore had done her best to keep the news off the TV and to stay inside since Kaliyah was with us for the week and the reporters were swarming. However, she was still trying not to allow the Blacks's bullshit to ruin her first week with her baby. By the time I'd left the house, she along with Kay Kay and Kaliyah were on a pallet in the living room watching movies.

When I left there weren't very many reporters out and they paid me no attention as I climbed in my car to pick up Quay. He'd been staying in since it was so close to Isis's due date, but he insisted on coming along tonight. Pulling up, he was already waiting out front with a blunt in his mouth, and he quickly tossed it before climbing in the passenger seat.

"What's up, big homie?" He grinned, dapping me up. His ass had been waiting on this day and wasn't even trying to hide his excitement.

"What's up, man?" Chuckling, I shook my head at his crazy ass and pulled off. It took us almost an hour to get to Hector's hideaway where the mayor was taking cover, and I immediately smiled upon seeing Hector's car there also. I parked down the road so they wouldn't notice me and slowly twisted my silencer on my gun, while Quay did the same with his.

"This feelin' like some *Grand Theft Auto* shit!" Still cheesing, he climbed out before I even could, making sure to close his door carefully. Taking the wooded way to try and hide our footsteps, we made the short trip up to the cabin-looking house. It was even more quiet than I thought it would be and I was worried they'd be able to hear us approaching. The closer we got though, I could hear music playing. It covered up our footsteps as we crept up the porch and stood on either side of the door. Silently, I counted up to three with my fingers and pushed the door open. I rushed inside where De'Niko Sr., Hector, and Hector's sister, Helena, stood. The two security men they had pulled their weapons while both Hector and Black shouted out different commands.

"What are you waiting for? Shoot them now!" Hector screamed, turning bright red in the face, and I smirked. Lowering my gun, I walked further into the room with Quay on the side of me, looking confused as hell.

"You see, they would, but niggas who ain't loyal don't deserve no loyalty. You thought I ain't know about you and this nigga side deals? You even pulled Bronx into yo' bullshit, but you gotta be quicker than that to get me!" I'd found out that

Hector had been trying to get me and Bronx to take each other out as a favor to my bum ass sperm donor. I wasn't sure what he was supposed to get out the deal, but at this point it didn't even matter. They were both going to die.

"Dominique! What do you think you're doing—"

"Oh, I'm making some shit right for a few people, *Dad*!" By now the two guards had moved to opposite sides of the room behind each man and before either could speak, they let their guns go off. De'Niko was hit in the head and Hector was shot twice, once in the neck and once in the chest.

"Yo, what the fuck?" Quay shouted, looking between each of the bodies as the guards placed their guns into their hands. I hadn't told him shit about what was going on, and the surprise on his face was definitely worth it. Clearing her throat, Helena stepped over her brother's body and reached out her hand.

"I don't think we've met. I'm Helena," she introduced herself with a smile, and he looked at us baffled but slowly shook her hand. "What took you so long? They were beginning to get restless."

"My bad, it was hard to find this muhfucka." I shrugged, tucking my gun back in my waist.

"Well, I'll be in touch." Snapping her fingers, she walked out the door, and a few minutes later the security followed her out. Once we were alone Quay's jaw was still on the floor, before a slow grin spread across his face.

"Nigga, you couldn't tell me about this shit?" he asked, walking out alongside me.

"Nah, that look on yo' face was priceless, but I wasn't sure if Helena was actually going to go through with it until we pulled up," I told him, locking and shutting the door.

"Big muhfuckin' homie!" he laughed as we made our way back to the car.

"You better know that shit too!" I agreed, pulling back off.

It took the police a week to find De'Niko and Hector's bodies, and from the scene they immediately ruled it a double homicide. They figured the two met up to talk about the trouble they were in and both pulled their weapons, killing one another instantly. Now that their case was closed, the last Black standing was going to take the fall for their illegal dealings. He was currently out on bond but I had no doubt he'd be his ass right back in there. With his legal proceedings going on he'd asked Adore to keep Kaliyah for another week, but when the judge found out about his charges, she immediately granted Adore temporary custody.

Not having to worry about them had her a lot more carefree, or maybe it was because she finally had her daughter all to herself. Either way, I was just happy that she was happy. "Y'all ready to go? My mama said to be up there by seven." I ducked into the room where Adore was struggling to put Kaliyah's hair up into a ponytail, while Kay Kay's hating ass stood by recording.

"I'm almost finished," she grumbled, pulling the hair tie from her wrist with her teeth, and I just shook my head.

"We ain't gone never make it at this rate." Glancing at my watch, I saw we were already late for the soft opening of the new restaurant, and I knew my mama was going to kill me. "Here, let me finish this. You go finish getting dressed," I told her, and relief washed over her. Giving me a quick kiss, she disappeared out of the room while Kay Kay complained.

"No fair, Daddy, she was going to owe us ice cream if she messed up!"

"Y'all ain't right!" I fought hard not to bust out laughing while the girls fell into a fit of giggles. They'd been tag teaming the fuck out of me and Adore, and I knew the shit was only going to get worse the older they got. I finished the ponytail and left it hanging down her back with a black bow on top to match her dress. The soft opening was black tie so we had the girls matching the theme.

"What's so funny?" Adore came in fully dressed in a black off-the-shoulder dress that came down to her knees, with black red bottoms. I'd bought her a diamond necklace and matching studs that gave her an elegant look since her hair was piled on top of her head, giving full view of her face and neck.

"Oooh, you look so pretty Mommy!" Kaliyah gushed before catching herself with a hand over her mouth. Up until this moment she'd been calling Adore by her name and since she'd wanted it to come naturally, Adore hadn't tried to force her.

"It's okay baby, thank you. You girls look very pretty too!" Adore got choked up, barely able to get the words out as she hugged a still stunned Kaliyah. We locked eyes over her head and I grinned, knowing how happy she was to finally be called mommy.

"Ayite, come on y'all, the car waiting." I clapped, snatching their attention, and they all ran to get their coats on. I planned to get fucked up and be knee deep in some pussy by the end of the night, and I didn't want having to drive to be in the way. Especially since both our mamas were likely to argue over who'd get to take the girls home.

As soon as we pulled up to the new restaurant there were camera flashes and microphones being stuck in our faces. The event planner had a red carpet laid out for the night and any and every magazine and newspaper in attendance.

"Oh my gosh! It's Adore Wallace, co-owner and manager of Pam's! You look amazing! Who do you have on tonight?" one of the interviewers slipped and said, making Adore's smile falter. I knew she was completely blindsided, and if I was an asshole I'd make the big-mouth reporter get escorted out. My OG had come up with the idea to have Adore as part owner since technically it would be her restaurant also. I hadn't known that she'd been helping my mama with her books and saving her money for some time. Her business degree had certainly come in handy, and since she didn't want to have to try and balance her time between here and Pam's one, then it was perfect for her.

Slipping my arm around her waist, I snuck and discreetly whispered, "Say thank you and that you're wearing Gucci." Still stunned, she looked up at me blinking, and I had to laugh. Shorty was just about in shock and couldn't get the words out even though her lips were moving. Since she was stunned into silence, I took over, knowing how easy it was to become distracted by a fine ass man like myself. When the lady realized she may not get anything out of her, she turned her attention on me.

"Dominique—I mean Heavy," she quickly corrected herself. "Are you excited about the opening and your girl getting the top spot?"

"I'm actually very thankful for the opportunity to be surrounded by two of the most beautiful and savvy business-women in the Chicago area," I said, flashing a charming smile that had the interviewer flushed. Ushering Adore further down the red carpet, she eventually got it together and was able to answer questions and speak, while the girls twirled and took advantage of all the cameras on them. When we finally made it inside, our OGs were standing near the entrance waiting on us. While Deb took the girls, my mama took Adore off to begin prepping the restaurant for the guests to arrive, and I grabbed one of the passing glasses of champagne and met Quay over in the corner. He stood hovering over Isis, who looked ready to push, as she sat with an annoyed look on her face. He'd been making sure to stay close to her and when he couldn't he had someone on her to make sure she wasn't overexerting herself.

"What's up, bro?" he asked as soon as I was close enough to hear him over the music playing.

"What's up?" I bent to give Isis's mean self a kiss on the cheek. "Hey Isis."

"Hey, where'd my girl rush off too?" she wanted to know, looking around.

"Oh, she's already been put to work." Nodding, she went back to scrolling on her phone, and I looked to Quay to figure out what her problem could've been. "What's up with her?"

Laughing, he took a sip of his champagne and nodded toward the other corner in the room where the staff from my OG's other restaurant stood. They were off tonight so they were in attendance as guests, and it looked like they had their sights set on Quay since I was off the market. "They been circling like vultures no matter how close I sit to her ass, and you know women always notice thirsty bitches," he cracked, and I chuckled. Some shit never changed.

A couple of hours later the night was over and had gone off without a hitch. Just like I'd suspected, the girls ended up going home with Adore's mama and I spent the rest of the evening diving in Adore's walls.

CHAPTER TWENTY-ONE
QUAY

After getting rid of the Blacks and Hector's bitch ass, Heavy and me began working with his sister Helena, and I had to admit that I fucked with her way more than her weird ass brother. The money had been rolling in and I was able to get me and Isis a bigger house that I planned to present to her after she had our son. She'd been on her best behavior since I found out about her sneaking her ass off to work in her store. Thankfully, the online thing worked out good and she'd been making a killing just from the comfort of our home. I hired her an assistant and even made myself available to help out whenever she needed me, which kept her from doing too much.

I'd just gotten back from dropping off some packages for her at the post office since her assistant, Ashley, had the day off. Shorty was one week past her due date, and when she wasn't getting on my nerves about wanting my son out of her, then she was trying to wobble her round ass to the basement to pack packages for shipment. I'd just accepted that my girl was a workaholic, and I hoped that my son's presence would eventually sit her the fuck down.

"Ice, where yo' big ass at!" I shouted when I came through the door, even though I already knew. I could already hear her slippers shuffling across the kitchen floor, and a second later she appeared in the doorway with a frown. Even looking irritated as fuck, she was still fine as hell to me.

"I told you to stop sayin' that!" she grumbled, but her eyes instantly lit up seeing the strawberry milkshake in my hand. "Oooh, is that mine?"

"Nope, I grabbed this on the way home. If you wanted one you should've said something. You do any other time." The lie had the smile sliding right off her face, and she looked like she wanted to slap the shit out of me. "Awww, I'm just playin' baby, this yours." Holding the shake out, I made my way across the room and handed it to her, kissing her still pouting lips until she kissed me back.

"You play too much, Quay." She was already slurping as she turned and headed back into the kitchen with me hot on her heels. Standing behind her, I rubbed my son, sending him into a kicking frenzy as she stood at the microwave watching her leftovers from Ms. Pam's spin on the tray. I swear it didn't make no sense how much the baby had her eating. According to the doctor he was going to be big too, at least nine pounds, which had her nervous, but she wasn't nervous enough to stop being obsessed with food.

I kissed her neck as the last few seconds ran out, rocking her body with mine as she moaned. I didn't know if it was because of me, the milkshake, or the food almost being ready, but I was going to pretend it was my kisses that had her purring. At least that's what I thought until she got real loud, and the next thing I knew, her water broke all over my damn Timbs.

"Oh shit! I think that was my water!" she screamed, trying to look between her legs while my face twisted.

"Nigga, what you mean you think? It better had been yo' water!" I fussed, stepping back slightly to see for myself. It was definitely time for her to deliver and my eyes bucked. "Come on, let's go get cleaned up so we can go up to the hospital." I held her arm to make sure she didn't slip. When we got to the stairs I realized how dumb it was that I didn't have a full bath on the first floor. Cursing, I lifted her bridal style and carried her up the stairs and frowned, seeing that her ass still had the damn milkshake. When we got to the landing, I set her back down and we headed into the master bath. I cut the shower on, while she stood in the middle of the floor trying to finish her drink. After helping her out of her clothes and taking off mine, we took a quick shower and got dressed in some sweats. Once she was dressed she sat down on the bed and directed me to grab all of the essentials she wanted to take to the hospital while she called Adore and my mama. I ran everything down to the truck before coming back to get her.

"You ready for this?" I asked, grinning wildly because I was only hours away from holding my son, and she rolled her eyes, unable to stop herself from smiling too despite her discomfort.

"I been ready for the last two weeks!" she said dramatically, even though I knew she was dead ass. My mama had her trying all types of shit to make the baby come, from pineapple slices to castor oil, and nothing had worked. I figured that shit wouldn't because my little man knew when the fuck he wanted to come, I just was smart enough not to tell her ass that. "What you doin'? I ain't bouta give birth in the backseat! I can sit in the front!" She moved away from the back door I was holding open for her and opened the passenger door instead. I helped her up and ran around to the driver's side.

An hour later she was in a room pushing and trying to

squeeze my damn hand like Aunt Viv as I did my best to coach her through her contractions. I alternated between standing next to her to standing between her legs so I could see, and shed real nigga tears as my son's head slid out.

"Damn, you're doing so fuckin' good, baby. His head is already out!" I shouted excitedly.

"Does he have a lot of hair?" her crazy ass asked in between the panting she was doing.

"Umm, yeah." I didn't know for sure what I'd seen besides his little head, and she instantly mugged me irritably, causing the doctor to chuckle.

"How don't you knooooooowoow!"

"Isis, he's got a head full of beautiful hair, honey. You're doing so great, but I need one more big push, okay?" Dr. Jones said, and Isis smiled briefly before burying her chin in her chest and screaming loud as hell. It felt like everything went silent around me as my baby's cries filled the room and tears spilled out over my cheeks, seeing the doctor finally hold him up. "Congratulations, it's a boy!" She held him up high so Isis could see him, and she immediately began to cry.

"You did so good baby, he's perfect," I told her, unable to stop kissing her all over her face.

"I know right?" she blubbered, not taking her eyes off him. The doctor handed me the scissors to cut his umbilical cord, and they whisked him across the room to clean him up while the other nurses continued to work between Isis's legs. I stood right over them watching as they poked and prodded him, making sure they didn't do anything to hurt him, even though I wouldn't have known because he never stopped crying until they placed him in a baby blue blanket and put him in my arms. He fit perfectly and I couldn't stop looking down into his tiny face that was the spitting image of mine. "Can I see my baby? I am the one who did all the work," Isis huffed from across the room. They'd finally finished cleaning her up also, but I still took my time carrying him over. I was trying to savor every minute I could.

"Naaah, I did all the work. That's why he look just like me," I teased, and she sucked her teeth, reaching her arms out for him. Reluctantly, I handed him over and she gushed and snuggled against his face. Besides him entering the world, this was the most beautiful thing I'd ever seen, and I instantly got choked up as a knock sounded at the door and our family rushed in.

"Congratulations!" they all shouted.

"Oh my, look at all that hair!"

"He's sooooo cute! Baby, I want one!" Adore nudged Heavy and he mugged me. I wasn't even about to take the blame for the baby fever my little man was going to give everybody. Even my mama was looking like she wanted to take her eggs out of retirement. They all ended up staying for about an hour before finally heading home, and Isis fell her tired ass to sleep, leaving me up with my son. She'd insisted on naming him upon seeing him since I didn't want to pass off my ghetto ass name, and we'd decided to name him Micah. It fit perfectly, and as I sat holding him I could already imagine yelling at his little bad ass to stop running in my house. The thought had me laughing aloud, and his face twitched into a small smirk like he knew exactly what I was thinking. He already had my sense of humor. I held on to my son until it was time for him to eat and I didn't have no choice but to hand him over to his mama, but I was ready to get him right back. Isis wasn't even tripping though because he'd tired her the fuck out and all she wanted to do was sleep. She deserved all the rest in the world after giving me the most perfect gift.

EPILOGUE
ADORE

TWO YEARS LATER...

"You look good as fuck. Won't you come back to bed." Heavy's nasty ass had me blushing as I put my earrings in. He'd already kept me up half the night knowing that we both would need to get up early, and there was no way I was getting back in the bed with him.

"Hell no, we still need to go wake up the girls and show the decorators where everything is supposed to go, set up the food..." I ran down the list of things we needed to get done before our guests arrived and he groaned, covering his face with a pillow.

"Come on, I'm just tryna stick the tip in." He looked up with a cocky grin, and I was already shaking my head.

"This is what happened last time you stuck the tip in." I pointed at my huge belly and used air quotes, making him bust out laughing.

"Shiiit, well now you ain't gotta worry about that happenin' again. We just gone be a little late." He shrugged,

and I rolled my eyes at his ass and left him right there begging. The girls were already hard sleepers, and it would take a good fifteen minutes just to get them fully awake. I waddled into Kay Kay's room and pulled her covers completely off so she couldn't pull them back on and shook her shoulder while calling her name.

"Wake up, Kay Kay, we gotta get dressed for the party. Kay Kay!" She immediately reached for the cover I'd taken and sat up when she didn't feel it near her. "Ohhh, you're up! Good morning baby, it's time to get dressed!"

"Morning Madore." Yawning, she swayed before finally climbing out of bed to get ready for the day. She'd been living with me and Heavy full time since Sha'ron never came out of the coma she was in. It was really hard on her for a while, and in some ways it was still hard. She didn't want to feel like she was replacing her mother with me, which was why she called me Madore, and I loved it. She was acknowledging me as her mama and it still made her feel as though she wasn't disrespecting Sha'ron. Running a hand over her head, I gave her a kiss on her forehead and left to go wake up Kaliyah. She was the hardest of the two to wake up, which was why I always saved her for last. Going across the hall to her room, I snatched off her covers and gave her a shake, also adding a couple of splashes of water to her face.

"Wake up, Kali! Come on, get up, we gotta get dressed for the day!" She jumped up gasping like I'd poured the water in her face as usual, and I just shook my head at her crazy little self. I'd won full custody of Kaliyah after De'Niko went to prison for embezzlement, among other things. For a while his mama tried to fight for custody since Farrah immediately left upon his guilty verdict and never looked back. I actually still had a problem with her for basically abandoning my child after all that performative shit she'd done. It was all "that's my daughter" and "I'm the only mother she knows," only for her to wash her hands of Kaliyah the minute she had the chance to. *Fucking bitch!* It was all for the better though, because Kali was much happier here with us.

"I'm up, Ma," she growled, sitting up with her eyes still closed, and I held in a laugh at how grumpy she always was in the morning. Giving her a kiss that she immediately wiped off, I headed downstairs. We were hosting a gender reveal and the people doing the decorations would be arriving any minute. Just as I reached the landing the bell rang, and I hurried to let them in. Ms. Pam came next with a few staff members carrying trays of food and I showed them where to set it up in the kitchen. I bounced between the kitchen and the backyard, directing everybody on what to do. By the time they'd finished setting up the tiki theme in the backyard Heavy was coming down, fully dressed in the blue polo shirt and khaki shorts he'd picked out for the day since he wanted a boy. While I had on a pink two-piece t-shirt and skirt set because I obviously wanted a girl.

"Hey ladies," he greeted everybody with that sexy ass smile before slipping his arms around me waist and kissing me like nobody was around.

"Well damn," I heard a few of the waitress's mumble, and I couldn't even be mad. Even after two years I still grew weak in the knees messing around with him. Shuddering, I wiped my lip gloss from his lips and finished setting up the napkins. The doorbell rang and I shooed him away to go get it.

"Bestie!" Before I even heard Isis, I heard my bad ass nephew's little feet scuffling across the floor. He was the true definition of the terrible twos. "No Micah, don't touch that!" she shouted next, and I knew he was in there messing with the figurines on my table. I was glad when the girls came running down the stairs after hearing his name and immediately scooped him up so they could take him in our finished basement to play. I'd made sure the basement den was Micah proof, meaning there wasn't shit down there he could reach or break, so that was his main location whenever he came over.

"Aye, you gone stop tryna send my son to baby jail." Quay entered the kitchen holding my niece Mia. Now Mia was the cutest with her little fat butt, but then again, she wasn't crawling yet either. She was the definition of a hip baby because she stayed on somebody's hip.

"You know the drill when his bad ass come over, so don't play." I mugged him and he cracked up laughing.

"My nigga break a couple things and all of a sudden he banned!"

"A couple things my ass. He broke my whole coffee table and everything on it," I corrected as he scratched the back of his head. He and Isis both knew Micah was bad as fuck, and you would've never known seeing him at the hospital.

"That's old as hell."

"Nigga, that shit happened last month!" This time he shut up because he knew he had no dog in this fight.

"Don't be up in here bad mouthin' my baby." Isis came in next looking gorgeous in a similar skirt as me, except hers was in blue since she wanted me to have a bad ass boy too.

"If you call tellin' the truth bad mouthin', then hey." I shrugged and she cracked up. At least she could admit that Micah's ass was bad. Quay, on the other hand, thought he could do no wrong. "Hey boo."

"Hey girl." She gave me a hug and went to wash her hands so she could help out. The last people to arrive were a few people from Pam's number two and the girls who worked at the bakery truck service I owned. I'd started my own business and had three trucks that catered to just the dessert needs. It was an idea that Heavy helped me come up with after he saw how well my deserts were selling out at both restaurants.

Heavy eventually came and snatched me up out the kitchen to actually enjoy the party. Even the girls came up with bad ass Micah and played a few games before he finally went down for a nap. Before I knew it, it was time to announce what we were going to have. My mama and Ms. Pam both knew but had been sworn to secrecy, and they walked the poppers over to us with sneaky smiles on their faces.

"Ooooh, y'all look like y'all up to something," I noted while Heavy just laughed.

"It's okay baby, whatever it is, it's gonna be perfect," he said, distracting me with a kiss, and I swooned.

"Aye, cut that shit out and get to it!" Quay shouted from somewhere in the crowd of people that surrounded us, and I raised my middle finger, making everybody laugh. We all counted down from five before we twisted the bottoms of our poppers and blue smoke erupted from the canisters. As much as I'd been complaining, I couldn't help squealing with joy right along with everybody else at the news that we were going to be having a boy. Heavy wrapped me up in a hug and lifted me off my feet as my eyes filled with tears. I'd worked really hard to get to this place and to feel deserving of the things I'd accomplished. I was in such a good place with the man of my dreams, the career of my dreams, and my children that it was crazy. It had taken me buying every dream a bum nigga sold me to finally get my dream come true.

The End.

ALSO BY J. DOMINIQUE